The James V. Brown Library
of Williamsport
and Lycoming County
Williamsport, Pennsylvania 17701
(570) 326-0536

BONANZA GULCH

BONANZA GULCH

Matt Stuart

Thorndike Press • Chivers Press
Thorndike, Maine USA   Bath, England

This Large Print edition is published by Thorndike Press, USA and by Chivers Press, England.

Published in 2000 in the U.S. by arrangement with Golden West Literary Agency.

Published in 2000 in the U.K. by arrangement with Golden West Literary Agency.

U.S. Hardcover 0-7862-2573-4 (Western Series Edition)
U.K. Hardcover 0-7540-4182-4 (Chivers Large Print)
U.K. Softcover 0-7540-4183-2 (Camden Large Print)

The text of this Large Print edition is unabridged.
Other aspects of the book may vary from the original edition.

Set in 16 pt. Plantin by Minnie B. Raven.

Printed in the United States on permanent paper.

British Library Cataloguing-in-Publication Data available

Library of Congress Cataloging-in-Publication Data

Stuart, Matt, 1895–
    Bonanza Gulch / Matt Stuart.
      p.   cm.
    ISBN 0-7862-2573-4 (lg. print : hc : alk. paper)
    1. Large type books.   I. Title.
  PS3515.O4448 B66   2000
  813′.52—dc21   00-028680

BONANZA GULCH

I

DEATH FOR TREASURE

The higher the road climbed into these
Shawmut Mountains the rougher it became,
and the lurching and jolting of the stage was
doing the lately healed gunshot wound in Jim
Teague's side no good at all. He wished now
that he'd taken his chances up on top; for
though the old thoroughbrace Concord was
loaded to the last thin inch with gold-hungry
humans, up on top a man could have moved
around at least a little, and so eased the jabbing torment of muscles and nerves but re-
cently ripped and torn and not yet firmly
knitted again. As it was, jammed almost to
breathlessness against the off side of the
stage's interior, all Teague could do was set
his teeth and bear it.

It helped some to steal a glance now and
then at the girl on the seat facing him. She
was definitely a nice girl and, just as definitely, out of place among this rough-and-
ready lot of gold seekers. For men argued in
loud voices and spilled profanity carelessly.
Then there was the sleek-looking tinhorn

sitting next to the girl. He had made several attempts to draw her into conversation, but without success, for she turned her head away and paid him no attention at all. But the fellow persisted and Teague could see the helpless indignation burn in her cheeks, saw her eyes flash and saw her bite at her lips.

Teague put out a foot and jammed a high, hard bootheel down on the tinhorn's instep. The tinhorn flinched and said sharply, "Watch yourself! That's my foot you're tromping on!"

Teague stared at him coldly. "Yeah? Well, I meant it to be."

The tinhorn had black eyes in a pale gambler's face and they fumed angrily. But under the steady impact of Teague's glance they turned shifty.

"The lady," went on Teague, "prefers to be left alone."

The tinhorn hunkered back, sulky but subdued. The girl gave Teague a steady glance out of clear, level eyes and in that look lay her unspoken thanks. Teague inclined his head gravely, then turned his attention to the passing country.

This was a raw and wild wilderness, a land of long running ridges, of deep and shadowy gorges, and of lofty, timbered crests that reached and climbed until they turned black with distance. Spring was in the air and in every gorge white water foamed and raced.

For hours there had been no slightest break in the steady, grinding ascent, but now at last the road began to level out and win its way through a pass, with dark timber close at hand and gray, storm-riven rock rims beyond, where, in crevice and pocket, snow still lay banked. The air was thin and brisk and keen.

The pass was not a long one, though it marked the backbone of the mountains, and soon the road began pitching downward in a series of abrupt switchbacks. It was at the sharp angle of one of these that a startled, growling curse came down from the driver's box while the stage lurched and swayed to a stop, brake blocks squealing under suddenly applied pressure.

Men scrambled down from the stage top and ran out ahead, trailing excited and profane conjecture. Those inside craned necks out of window and door, trying to see what this was all about. Jim Teague did better than that. He pulled himself forward and climbed out. Here was a chance to give that bad side a little relief.

Out there ahead stood another stage, the team swung until the entire conveyance stood almost crossways in the road. Men were grouped, staring at something on the ground. Teague marched his way up and pushed in close enough to see.

It was a dead man who lay there, dead long enough to have stiffened. A man who had been, Teague judged, a shotgun guard, for the sawed-off weapon of his trade lay on the ground under him. He'd been shot through the head.

Teague heard a tight drawn little gasp at his shoulder. He turned and saw the girl standing there, staring with wide, stricken eyes. One slim hand had been at her throat. Now it dropped to Teague's arm, a gesture entirely instinctive and unrealized.

"He — he's dead!" she murmured.

"Yes," answered Teague. "Very. You shouldn't be here, looking around. There may be more of them."

"There is," growled a burly miner. "The driver's on the far side of the stage, just as dead as this one."

The girl averted her head, turned away. Jim Teague went around to the other side. The driver of Teague's stage stood looking down at the man sprawled there.

"Tom Sarber," he said harshly. "As good a whip as ever climbed a wheel. Looks like him and his treasure guard never had a

10

chance. I'd been wonderin' what was makin' Tom late. We should have met him way down the other side of the mountains."

A man who'd been prowling off to the side of the road called, "Here's the treasure box — and empty!"

Teague had a look. The lock had been shot off the box. The finder of the box said, "Whoever pulled this holdup were pretty damn cool customers."

Teague moved out a little further and found where two horses had stood in the timber back from the road. Here also was something else, an empty revolver shell that had been tossed aside. The early spring's pale sun, cutting down through the timber, had picked out the glitter of it. Teague scooped it up and his eyes pinched slightly at the corners as he examined it.

"Yeah," he murmured to himself. "Cool customers, all right. But careless. For the .44 Russian isn't too common a gun. Yet, it's no affair of mine." He flipped the empty shell aside and went back to the stage.

A man was saying, "What do you figure happened to the passengers of this stage?"

The driver of Teague's stage answered. "Likely enough Tom Sarber didn't have any passengers. Last three runs I've made out of Bonanza Gulch I rode an empty stage. Right

11

now folks are headin' into Bonanza Gulch, not away from it. Headin' out will come later when the diggin's begin to fade and word comes in of another placer strike somewhere else."

While speaking, the driver was looking around, and his glance settled on Teague. "You got the look of horse savvy about you, friend. Think you could ribbon this team and stage back to Bonanza Gulch? Sure can't leave it here, or Tom Sarber and his shotgun guard, either."

"I think I can handle things for you," Teague told him briefly. "Have those two loaded inside."

Teague checked swiftly over the hookup of the team, gathered up the trailing reins and climbed to the driver's box. Grim-faced miners loaded the two dead men inside. The driver of the inbound stage lifted a call.

"There's room for some of you folks on this rig. Won't hurt to lighten up my load a mite."

The girl had gone back to the other stage, head bent. The tinhorn gambler stood by the step, plainly intent on helping her to her place. He started to speak to her, but the girl turned swiftly away, came back and looked up at Jim Teague. "Would you mind if I rode with you, up there?" she asked.

Teague shrugged. "Plenty of room."

She came up, scrambling lithely, and settled herself beside Teague a trifle breathlessly. A couple of men came over from the other stage and took places. Teague spoke to the team, got them straightened out and moving and swung the Concord far enough aside to let the other stage pass, the driver yelling across at him, "Wide place just a little above where you can turn around."

Teague found the place, made the turn and went rolling down the switchbacks after the other stage, riding the brake with a jamming boot whenever the rig started to climb up the haunches of the wheelers.

His tender side was feeling better and some of the taut bleakness went out of his face. It was a face thinned by several weeks in bed, while that wounded side had healed. The mahogany stain of years of wind and sun was burned too deeply to have faded entirely, but there was a hint of pallor underneath. The jaw angle was gauntly strong, the lips somewhat repressed and harsh. Gray eyes, slightly sunken, looked out at the world with a hard aloofness, a sort of sardonic and calculating skepticism of men and their motives.

Teague's clothes had seen better days and, literally, all he possessed in the world was on

13

his back. It had taken his last cent to buy a seat on the stage in to Bonanza Gulch. Once he had owned a cow hand's outfit, horse and saddle gear, a rifle and a six-shooter. Plus seventy-five dollars in his jeans. That was how things were when he sat into the poker game at Timber Lodge.

When the game had ended abruptly, there was a dead gambler on the floor, while Teague was trying to hold himself erect with a left hand braced on the table top while his right held his smoking gun. The gambler hadn't been quite as nifty with his hide out derringer gun as he'd been with the cards. But he had come close — awful close. He had put both slugs from that wicked, snub-nosed, doubled-barreled little weapon into Jim Teague's side, not two inches apart. Teague had thrown but a single slug, yet he had placed that precisely under the third button of the gambler's fancy silk shirt.

When completely certain that the gambler was dead, Teague had folded up himself. The doctor in Timber Lodge had done a first-rate job, but in his eyes Jim Teague was just another tough, drifting rider and a fee was a fee. Besides which, it cost hard money to hold down a hotel bed for better than a month while the wounds healed and some measure of strength returned. So, in the end, horse and riding gear, money and everything else went.

Rupe Caldwell's letter had caught up with Teague the day he left that hotel bed. Rupe was in Bonanza Gulch and the letter promised something which Jim Teague was mightily interested in just then — easy money and plenty of it.

The letter was a complete surprise, for Teague hadn't seen Rupe Caldwell in over a year. He had, in fact, almost forgotten that Caldwell had ever existed. He had known the man only as another of the wild, reckless bunch that had ridden with him for Garr Paden, back in the days of the Wagon Wheel River range war. There had been nothing permanent about those days, nothing certain — not even life itself. Men rode in to the outfit, men rode out. Some of them had died during the riding. Rough days, rough trails, rough men.

Rupe Caldwell had drawn Garr Paden's pay for little more than six weeks. And then one day, coming out of a gun smoke session with a bullet burn across his jaw, Caldwell had declared that there were easier and more certain ways of earning a living, and so had drawn his time. Which was the last Jim Teague had seen or heard of him until that letter came along.

15

Teague remembered Caldwell as a big man, florid, restless and talkative; and tough enough when he wanted to be. Caldwell hadn't pulled out of the Wagon Wheel River trouble because he was afraid. Instead, as he'd said on quitting, he saw no sense in laying his life on the line for forty a month and found, in another man's interests. Which rated, Teague had to admit, as pretty hard-headed judgment.

"If I'm going to risk stopping a slug," was what Caldwell had said, "I might as well do it while trying to work out a good stake for myself, instead of fattening up somebody else."

The stage rolled out the last of the switchbacks and then lined out across a lessening slope along the road which cut its way between solid stands of big timber. The afternoon was shortening and where the slanting rays of the spring sun struck through, golden mists smoked and coiled.

The girl beside Jim Teague had not spoken a word. She sat lithe and erect, balancing easily to the groaning sway and lurch of the stage, looking straight ahead, the crisp bite of the open air laying a thin stain of color across the softly moulded contours of her face. Her mouth was grave and in her

16

eyes lay the shadow of the day's grimness.

Teague spoke abruptly. "You've kin in Bonanza Gulch?"

She met his glance before answering. "Yes. My father. Why do you ask?"

Teague shrugged. "From what I've heard, Bonanza Gulch is a pretty tough camp. We've seen enough today to believe that. But as long as you've a father there, it will be all right."

Her soft chin tilted. "I can take care of myself."

They came upon the Gulch suddenly, for it lay just beyond the edge of timber which ended abruptly, without any preliminary thinning. It was like breaking through a wall. The camp lay along a low, slow-curving benchland above some long running flats which stretched on either side of a brawling stream. These flats were alive with activity. Water-soaked and mud-smeared miners toiled furiously there, popping in and out of shallow shafts and pot holes for all the world like an army of bedeviled gophers.

Piles of raw earth and newly dug gravel mounded the level face of the flats and here and there the sun struck up glittering flashes from tool surfaces scoured bright from steady use. Small tents pegged their shapes here and there, and there was a drift of wood smoke in the air from open cooking fires.

The main camp was a rough-and-ready outfit, with its single street winding crookedly and its buildings thrown together with no semblance of ordered layout in mind. Men seemed to have built wherever chance or fancy struck.

There were a few solid, log-built structures, but for the most it was anything that would in some part hold out the weather. There were buildings of hastily and rough sawn boards, put together while the lumber was dripping green, and which were now warped and twisted, the cracks covered with strips of canvas, or with tin cans hammered flat and nailed on, or with daubs of dry and flaking mud. There were structures half of wood and half of canvas, and some that were of canvas alone. It was a new camp, rough and ugly, with little more than a year of life behind it, and a future measured only by the gods of chance and the amount of placer gold which lay in those flats beside the stream.

The leading stage had pulled up before one of the better log buildings and was already discharging its passengers when Jim Teague brought his team to a halt beside it. There were a lot of men milling up and down the street and a number of them had begun to crowd around, wondering at the sight of two stages pulling in together. The story of the holdup quickly became general news and an ominous growl went up.

A miner yelled, "I shipped a good stake of gold out on that stage. What this camp needs is a miners' court that'll stretch a few necks!"

Another miner warned the angry one. "Better watch that talk, Barney Foxx. Else you'll be getting a knife in your back the same as Duff Sherrill did when he suggested the same thing."

The girl at Jim Teague's side had been leaning forward, eyes searching the crowd anxiously. Now, as the words of the miners carried to her, she stiffened as though struck with a whip, and an anguished cry broke from her.

"No — no! Not Dad! Not a knife — !"

She would have scrambled down headlong if Teague hadn't caught her by the arm. "Easy!" he warned brusquely. "This is a tall stage. I'll give you a hand."

She turned on him, ghost-white, her eyes dark with terror. "Let me go! You heard what that man said? Dad — he's been — !"

"Easy!" said Teague again, his tone gentling. "We'll find out about this."

Teague climbed down, then helped the frantic girl, lifting her bodily from the top of the wheel. He had marked the man in the crowd, so now pushed a way over to him, and spoke curtly.

"A minute, friend. You just said something about a man named Sherrill — Duff Sherrill."

The miner looked at Teague suspiciously. "Suppose I did?" he growled with a show of surliness. "I didn't stick the knife in him."

The girl's voice became a thin wail. "But you don't understand! Duff Sherrill is my father. He's not — not — ?"

The miner's manner changed instantly. "Lordy! Your father, miss? Well now, it'll sure make Duff get well faster to have you around."

"Then he's not — dead?"

"Not him! Duff had a mighty close call, but he's a tough old rooster and is coming along in good shape."

She fairly whimpered in her relief. "Where is he?"

"In the cabin where him and Les Jardeen live."

"Mind showing us the place?" asked Teague.

"Of course not. Come on!"

They worked their way through the crowd

and along the street, turning away past a sprawling building that was half log and half sawn board structure. Somewhere in it a piano was banging discordantly. The miner pointed at a cabin which stood on the outer rim of the benchland. "That's it."

Teague thanked him, then strode fast to keep up with the hurrying girl. They were almost at the cabin when the door opened and a young fellow stepped out. He was well set up, with a thinly handsome face and a long mane of tawny hair. He stared at Teague and the girl, profoundly startled. The girl spoke swiftly.

"I'm Janet Sherrill. Is my father in there?"

The young miner, recovering from his surprise, nodded. "Go right in, miss. Me, I'm Les Jardeen. Lordy! The cabin's a mess. If I'd known you were coming I'd have done some cleaning up. Now this is going to do Duff all manner of good."

The girl wasn't even listening. She ran into the cabin and Jim Teague heard her soft cry. "Dad! Oh, Dad — this is Janet —!"

Teague stared at the door for a moment with enigmatic eye, then turned to Les Jardeen. "You're a pardner of Sherrill's?"

"Not exactly a pardner. But I've been sharing his cabin. I'd call myself a pretty good friend of his. Why?" There was a

21

thread of truculence in the young miner's tone and manner.

"This is a tough camp for a girl like Miss Sherrill to be in," said Teague. "And she's all lady. Let's everybody remember that."

Teague turned and went back to the center of town. There was still a crowd milling around the door of the stage station. Teague worked his way through them and into the station. In a corner of the place two still figures lay, and a short, rather stout man with a broad, blunt jaw was covering them with blankets. The man's blue eyes were bright with a banked anger. That same anger was in his voice as he spoke to a lank, spare man who carried a holstered gun at his hip and a star on his left shirt front.

"I don't want any more excuses, Riker. I want results. You say you were sent in to Bonanza Gulch by Judge Ormond of Timber Lodge to administer the law. All right, let's see some of that law which will benefit a few others besides Rupe Caldwell. Jake Howe can tell you exactly where the holdup took place. Whoever pulled it must have left some sign. That sign will lead somewhere. In short, get out there and do something!"

Jake Howe, driver of the stage in from Timber Lodge, said, "Right in the angle of the fourth switchback this side the pass was where we found things, Riker."

Sheriff Wade Riker said in a thin, cold way, "I'll ride up and have a look around. Sure, I'll probably find some sign, but how far I'll be able to follow it is anybody's guess. You forget that this is a damn big and wild country. It's no ten acre cornfield. And I'm no miracle worker."

He turned and stamped out. Teague got the impression of a cold, dark face and black eyes fuming with anger.

Jake Howe said, "This is the feller who brought in Tom Saber's stage, Ben. Mebbe you can talk business with him."

The stout man looked at Teague. He nodded. "This affair leaves me short a driver, friend. You can have the job if you want it."

Teague shook his head. "Thanks, but I'm not interested." He turned to Jake Howe. "The young lady must have had some luggage. Where is it?"

There were two well-stuffed grip sacks in the luggage boot of the Timber Lodge stage. Jake Howe turned them over to Teague, who carried them out to that cabin at the edge of the benchland. At Teague's knock it was Les Jardeen who came out.

"Miss Sherrill's luggage," said Teague.

He was turning away when the girl darted

past Jardeen. "Wait!" she called, "You've been very kind. I want to thank you, Mr. —"

"Teague. Jim Teague. No thanks necessary, Miss Sherrill. I hope you found your father in good shape?"

He knew that she had, for the taut strain was gone from her face and eyes, and color was back in her cheeks. She had taken off her hat and traveling coat. She made an appealing picture in the eyes of a lonely man. A soft laugh touched her lips.

"He was gruff as a bear at first, saying I had no business coming to a camp like this. But now I know he's glad I came."

The grimness about Teague's lips softened a trifle. "I'm sure he is."

He touched his hat and again returned to town. So much for that. Now he had to line up his own affairs. The first thing to do was locate Rupe Caldwell, if he was to eat and have a place to sleep this night. And Teague realized how much he needed both. It had been a long day and had taken a lot out of him. His legs were beginning to feel rubbery and his wounded side was aching. Toward these things he felt the impatient anger of a normally strong and tireless man over any suggestion of physical weakness.

He turned in at the door of the big, sprawling building where the piano still

24

hammered discordantly. A sign above the door of the place proclaimed it as the Big Nugget. It was fairly crowded along the bar and around the numerous poker tables. There was a faro layout, but it was closed to play just now. In a far rear corner was the piano and all the back end of the place was open for dancing, though deserted just now, except for the man at the piano.

He was a strange-looking sort, this man at the keyboard. Short almost to dwarfishness, he hunched close over the keys, while his fingers, stubby but amazingly agile, just now struck one jangling discord after another. His pallid, doughy features held a twisted bitterness. It was as though the man himself was full of inner discords that were finding outlet through his jabbing fingers.

But right after Jim Teague entered the place the piano went silent. For a man's voice echoed, high and harsh and angry.

"I tell you I'm goin' in to see Rupe Caldwell, and nobody is goin' to stop me. Get out of my way, Ides!"

There was a scattering of the crowd about the bar, leaving two men facing each other. One of these was a miner, shaggy and raw-boned. Facing him was a slender, almost dapper figure, faintly and mockingly smiling.

25

"Rupe can't be bothered, Dorgan. You saw him yesterday. The argument is settled as far as Rupe is concerned. Go on about your business!"

"My business is right in that side room," was the miner's savage retort. "There's a dirty, thievin' rat in that room and its name is Caldwell. Not he or anybody else can steal my claim and get away with it. I'm going in there and get that rat!"

The miner started forward. The dapper man rocked up on his toes. "Far enough, Dorgan!" he warned.

The next few moments were wickedly fast and deadly. The miner cursed and clawed an ancient bulldog revolver from the pocket of his coat. His purpose was direct, but in all other things he was slow and clumsy. He had the revolver only half clear when the dapper man whipped a gun from a shoulder holster and shot him dead. The miner was going down, in a breaking, crumpling fall, when the dapper man shot him a second time.

After the rumble of the guns faded, a long moment of silence held. It was broken by the slamming back of a door beyond the far end of the bar. It was Rupe Caldwell who stepped out. He seemed coldly calm.

"What is it, George?"

The dapper man backed up slowly, watching the crowd. "Dorgan," he said, across his shoulder. "Gunning for you, Rupe. I warned him off. But he went for his gun and pushed his luck too far."

A voice lifted from the silent crowd. "I can name others who'll be pushing theirs too far one of these days. Jack Dorgan was a good man, and honest."

The dapper man reared on his toes again, staring toward the voice. "You'll talk your way into a grave yet, Barney Foxx!"

"I've no gun on me, George Ides," came the steady retort. "So I doubt you'd dare murder me in daylight. And at night I'll be watchful."

A stir, then an ominous growl ran through the crowd. Another voice said, "That's tellin' the dirty killer, Barney. There's a limit to this sort of business. Our time will come. Now who'll be givin' me a hand to carry Jack Dorgan away?"

Several men pushed forward, gathered up the dead man and filed out. The dapper killer, George Ides, watched them coolly, that thin and mocking smile still on his face.

Jim Teague, quiet and impassive, eyes inscrutable, stood in guarded silence. He was no stranger to violent death. And he was thinking now that men died that way on the open range and they died that way in bar-rooms and gambling hells, driven by the same angers and greeds and cruelties no matter where they stood or what the background. Since they first walked the earth, men had fought and killed each other. And, he concluded cynically, they always would.

He turned his glance to Rupe Caldwell, who saw him at the same moment. For a moment Caldwell stared. Then he called, "Teague — Jim Teague!"

Teague walked over to meet him. Caldwell had his hand thrust out and he was beaming with all his old-time geniality.

"Man!" he exclaimed. "Am I glad to see you! I'd just about given up all hope of my letter reaching you. Jim, you couldn't have shown up at a more opportune time."

Teague shrugged, shaking hands. "A pretty rough time, it would seem, Rupe."

II

BONANZA GULCH

They sat in that side room of the Big Nugget, alone. Jim Teague listened while Rupe Caldwell talked.

"I'm remembering, Jim, the days when we rode together in that Wagon Wheel River range war. Tough men on both sides and none tougher than you. And smart. That's why I remembered you and wrote to you. I need tough, smart men. I can find plenty who are tough but not smart, and plenty who are smart but not tough. It is the combination I'm after."

"Maybe you overrate me, Rupe," drawled Teague. "I arrive here in Bonanza Gulch flat broke and weak as a cat, because I let a tinhorn gambler fool me with a hide-out gun. Such things shouldn't happen to a smart, tough man."

Caldwell laughed. "Broke, you say? Now we will fix that, quick!"

A squat iron safe stood in a corner of the room. Caldwell worked over it a moment then came back and tossed a fat little buck-

29

skin sack on the table, where it thumped heavily.

"Yours," said Caldwell carelessly. "About fifty ounces. That will buy things for you. There'll be one just like it every month if you tie in with me, Jim."

Teague hefted the gold poke, calculated swiftly. Caldwell hadn't lied in his letter. This was big money, all right. Teague leaned back in his chair.

"All right, let's have it. But remember, Rupe — I've got some conscience left."

Caldwell's genial laugh rang out. "The only time I was ever a fool was when I was risking my skin riding for Garr Paden at forty a month and found. Don't worry, man. The law is all on our side. Here's the story, short and sweet."

Caldwell paused long enough to light a stogie, while Teague studied him guardedly. The man hadn't changed much. Still with that hearty floridness of face, that agile tongue and ready laughter. A little fleshier, perhaps, which meant that he hadn't had any saddle work of late. Caldwell let out a cloud of smoke and went on.

"A prospector by the name of Carr made the first strike to start this camp. I heard it was rich and came in here. I had some money, enough to put together this building and set up in business. I've made money, for it is a rich camp, Jim. Last winter Andy Carr, being of that queer, restless breed all prospectors are, got the itchy foot again. With his kind, Jim, it seems to be the looking for and maybe finding, that lures them on and on. Keeping it after they've found it, is the least of their concern. Anyhow, Carr got the itch to start wandering again and he offered to sell me his discovery claim. It was a pickup at the price, so I grabbed it.

"Andy pulled out and Lord knows where he is now, tailing along after his burros, digging and scratching and looking. And I've settled down to getting out of that discovery claim all that's in it. Now then, in a strike like this in Bonanza Gulch, the location of most of the other claims, in particular the closely adjacent ones, stem from the discovery claim. When a man files on such a claim, he records it as being so many feet above or below discovery."

Teague nodded. "I know about that."

Caldwell rolled his stogie across his lips. "Fine. Well, if a man makes a gross error in his measurements, his title is invalid and the ground is open to anyone else who wants to record it, and record it properly. In other words, a claim recording has to be reasonably exact as to physical location, or it is meaningless. So, one of the first things I did after buying up Discovery was to check its limits and measurements carefully. The claim runs three hundred feet each way from the discovery stake, fronting the creek. And I found that number one above and number one below Discovery were way out of line. Number one below overlapped Discovery by a good hundred feet, while number one above lacked contacting Discovery by roughly the same distance. Which made both of the claim recordings invalid. So I moved in on them. Now," and here Caldwell shrugged, "there is pretty hell to pay."

Teague stirred. "Such as — ?"

"Former claimants making all kinds of threats and war talk. Accusing me of everything from baby stealing to bigamy."

"In their place," drawled Teague, "I'd probably feel the same."

Rupe Caldwell let his big laugh roll out. "Lord love you, so would I. As things stand though, I'm fully within my rights according to law, and I'd be a fool not to take advantage of that fact. Any time the law rules me as wrong, I'll move out."

"The kind of law that would settle that sort of thing is quite a long way from Bonanza Gulch, isn't it?" asked Teague dryly.

Caldwell shrugged. "That's the other fellow's hard luck, not mine. Look, Jim," Caldwell leaned on the table, his elbows spread. "You and I went through the Wagon Wheel River range war — or at least through a part of it. What was that war about? Land. Grass. Water. The things that Garr Paden claimed and that other men claimed, too. Range boundaries were in dispute, all that sort of thing. Who was wrong and who was right, Jim? When I left, who had control? Garr Paden. How'd he get it? By moving in and taking over. If he hadn't done that, somebody else would have. Who helped him move in? Guys like you and me, throwing smoke and eating it. Have you lost any sleep over your part of that deal?"

"Never gave it any thought," Jim Teague admitted. "It was the accepted order of things on that range. You rode for one outfit or you rode for another. And either way there was fighting to do."

"Exactly!" Rupe Caldwell brought a clenched fist down on the table. "Exactly, Jim. So what's the difference here? Well, I can tell you one big difference. There it was forty a month and found. Here it is fifty ounces of gold dust a month. And if the take warrants it, and I'm dead certain it will, I'll hike that ante. I'm putting sluice boxes on my three claims. I'm throwing a real crew of men on to the claims to really work that gravel. There will be thousands of dollars' worth of gold in those sluices at every cleanup. That kind of treasure rates guarding, and guarding well by men who are smart, by men who are tough, and by men I can trust."

"And you think I rate?" asked Teague.

"If I didn't, would I have sent out a letter to chase you all over the country? Man, I'm remembering you as I saw you and knew you along the Wagon Wheel River. So now you got the picture. How's it look to you?"

Teague stood up, stowing the heavy gold poke away. "Where can a man eat and sleep in this camp?"

"You're in luck," said Caldwell. "There's a spare bunk in my cabin. Come on!"

They went out into the main room of the Big Nugget. The place was virtually empty, for this was the twilight hour, when men were more intent on food than drink or gaming. A roustabout was lighting the several big hanging lamps of the place.

The street outside was equally empty. The air had turned bitter, for this was a high camp and spring but lately arrived. Smoke from fat pine fires sifted in pale layers up and down the world and touched the nostril pungently. A big freight outfit, lead wagon and back action heavily loaded, was just lumbering into town, late arrival from Timber Lodge.

Rupe Caldwell pointed to the freight wagons. "There's more ways of making big money in a camp like this than just digging it out of the ground, Jim. I can remember when Buck O'Connor started hauling supplies in here with a single team and an oversized spring wagon. Now he owns that big Merivale double hitch outfit and three more just like it, grinding steadily back and forth between here and Timber Lodge and all of them dropping dollars in Buck's pocket every turn of the wheels. Yeah, the world is full of big money for the man who can get his nose above saddle sweat or a patch of placer gravel."

"Maybe the smell of saddle sweat is its own reward to some," said Teague briefly. "And maybe shoveling gravel and looking for gold is the same with others. Some things in this world money can't buy, Rupe."

Caldwell chuckled, his hand tightening on Teague's arm. "You give me the gold, Jim — and I'll manage to buy what I want."

Caldwell's cabin was one of a group of three which stood a little apart from town on the upslope side. Light was already showing in the other two and Caldwell got a small lamp going while he showed Teague about this one. There was a pair of bunks against opposite walls of the place and Caldwell pointed to one of them.

"Yours, Jim. Make yourself at home. There's grub on the shelf yonder any time you want to cook up a meal for yourself." He eyed Teague with a swift glance, noting the way Teague's gaunt shoulders were hunched against the chill. "You need some new and warmer clothes, man. You can get them at the trading post, which is next to the stage station. And if you want to buy a meal, they serve fair grub at the hashhouse across from the trading post. Have yourself a good sleep tonight and I'll see you in the morning. Now I got things to do. A busy man, you know," he ended, grinning.

Jim Teague left a sizable part of that fifty ounce poke at the trading post, returning to the cabin with his arms loaded with bundles. He got a fire going in the stove. He heated water in a couple of buckets made from empty five gallon kerosene tins. He shaved, then stripped and soaped and sluiced himself down for a satisfactory bath. The touch of the hot water on his tender side was soothing and good. He got into new underwear, donned a blue wool shirt, trousers of dark corduroy and a pair of boots, all new and stout and warm. Finally, under the lamplight he cleaned the packing grease from a new Peacemaker Colt gun and tested the feel and action of the weapon.

He broke open a box of ammunition, plugged loads into five of the cylinder chambers of the gun, lowered the hammer on the empty sixth, then tucked the weapon inside the waist band of his trousers, slightly around on the left side. He donned a new corduroy coat, blanket-lined, picked up his hat, blew out the lamp and left the cabin.

The dark was heavy, the stars brilliant, and the chill of the night biting against the freshly shaven angles of his face. It got no deeper. A sense of well-being he hadn't known since before the shooting affair in Timber Lodge pervaded him, except that sheer hunger was a raw torment within him.

The big rush of the evening at the hash-house was past. Teague had the place to himself. The food was coarse and plain, but well cooked and savory. It took hold of Teague, drove the last trace of weakness out of him, softened the tautness about his lips. He was lingering over a final cup of coffee when the door opened and the short, bustling man who had offered him a job as stage driver, came in, taking a stool further along the counter, throwing a glance at Teague but not recognizing him, what with the changes a shave and bath and new clothes had made.

The waiter, when he put food in front of the stage agent, said, "Well, Ben — rough times an' gettin' rougher. You heard about Jack Dorgan?"

"I heard," was the growling answer. "Another good man gone. I tell you, Mitch — this thing is going to end up in a lynching bee they'll date time from."

"From what I heard, Dorgan didn't play it too smart," offered Mitch. "He goes bustin' into the Big Nugget, snortin' fire and war talk. George Ides warned him off, but instead of listenin', Dorgan tries to throw a gun. That was a fool move, Ben. No smart man tries to throw a gun on George Ides."

"Ides," snapped the stage agent, "is a low, rotten killer, just like Bully Girard, Curly Bolan and all the rest of those damned whelps Rupe Caldwell has surrounded himself with. But decent, honest men ain't going to stand for this sort of thing forever. I've seen my share of gold camps and I think I know the ordinary, hard-working miner pretty well. He's a long-suffering cuss and takes a lot of pushing around before he really catches fire. But when he finally does — look out! Mark my words, Mitch. There'll come a day of reckoning in this camp and it'll be a grim one, or my name ain't Ben App."

Mitch stirred uneasily. "Was I you, Ben, I wouldn't talk too loud or strong. It was that sort of thing that got Duff Sherrill a knife in the back."

"Maybe," mumbled Ben App, over a mouthful of food. "Maybe it was that, Mitch — and maybe it wasn't. I think Duff Sherrill got that knife mainly because he owns number one claim below Discovery, and because he's too much of a fightin' man to let Rupe Caldwell get away with his damn thievery. Soon as Duff can be fully up and around again, you'll see the fur fly. Of course, now that they got Jack Dorgan out of the way, Caldwell and his crowd won't have any trouble looting number one above Discovery. Dorgan had a mighty good claim, there. Barney Foxx says he figures number one above will turn out to be the richest claim in the Gulch. And when it comes to judgin' placer claims, they don't come any smarter than Barney."

Mitch changed the subject. "I hear Duff

Sherrill's girl has come to live with him. I hear she's pretty as a snow flower."

"A pretty girl and a mighty nice one," nodded Ben App. "This camp is no place for the likes of her, though. But Les Jardeen was telling me that old Duff has perked up amazing, now that the girl is with him."

"Les Jardeen," said Mitch scathingly, "is nice to look at. But he ain't what you'd call fast in the head. Barney Foxx says that when the Lord passed out the brains, Les Jardeen musta been hidin' in the oat box."

At the trading post, Jim Teague had exchanged some of his gold for specie, so now he paid his score and left the hashhouse. He went up to the Big Nugget and bought a cigar. Then he sauntered about the room, watching the poker games at this table and that. The faro layout was busy and the dealer was the tinhorn Teague had told off on the stage. The lookout was George Ides, dapper, cold-eyed, imperturbable.

The ugly, dwarfish man was at the piano and now smooth melody rippled out under the touch of his stubby fingers. Several couples were dancing in the back area, the girls painted and flounced, their partners for the most part heavy-booted miners with the mud and grime of the diggings still smeared on them. One of those dancing, Jim Teague recognized as Les Jardeen.

Teague's glance followed Jardeen and his partner, a slender, dark-eyed, not unhandsome girl. Other eyes, Teague noted, followed this same couple, for, whenever they circled near the piano, the little man at the keys would swing his head to watch them and then his pushed and ugly features would twist up, and stabbing discords would creep into the rippling beat of his music.

No one paid the slightest attention to Jim Teague as he moved quietly about, a tall man, somewhat gaunt, face hard-drawn and lean almost to hawkishness, gray eyes reserved and inscrutable. From time to time the high, shrill laughter of one of the dance hall girls cut through the normal hum of the place, which was a combination of shuffling feet, growling voices, clack of poker chips, and the measured beat of the piano.

At intervals, Teague saw three different men go into and come out of the door of that side room beyond the inner end of the bar. One of these was a big, hulking brute, red of hair and beard. Another, a smaller man, was swarthy and bullet-headed, his black hair close curled about his skull. The third was Wade Riker, the sheriff. When Riker came out he went over to the faro table and began to play.

Teague left the Big Nugget and went back to the cabin. The fire had gone out and the place was full of chill. Teague turned in immediately and lay in the quiet darkness, thinking. Not all were easy thoughts. He had heard things, he had seen things, but not nearly enough of anything to judge fully or for sure.

He knew men pretty well. He knew that many things influenced their opinions and motives. Personal gain was always a prime consideration. Little, futile men were always quick to brand big and successful ones as unscrupulous and full of thievery. Sometimes such claims were just, but just as often, definitely unjust. In the main the processes of law gave everybody a fair shake, though there were times when its very intricacies benefited a few at the expense of the many. Still and all, it was the law.

The things Jim Teague knew best were far away from this booming mining camp. The dust of cattle trails, the open, far running miles of grass and range; the creak of saddle gear, the feel of a staunch horse between his legs. There, too, did men take sides and have opposing opinions which brought on hatreds and conflict, charges and counter-charges. But it was a world and a language and mode of life which Teague knew intimately. Here, in this mining camp, it was a different language and there was much he did not know about it. Only the rumbling currents of human nature were the same and these currents reduced all men to the same common mold, and out of that sameness came the inevitable argument and conflict.

Of one thing, Teague was completely sure. He was once again well clothed, well fed and warmly bunked. These were the fundamental needs of all life, concrete things which really counted. For the present nothing else really mattered.

Sleep was moving in upon him and related thought faded. But, strangely enough, one picture lingered, bright and clear at the last edge of consciousness. The swaying, jouncing seat of a stage, with a slender, clean-eyed girl beside him . . .

Jim Teague had been asleep for hours when, well after midnight, Rupe Caldwell came in and took the other bunk.

The placer diggings proper of Bonanza Gulch stretched up and down both sides of Vining Creek for a distance of some three miles, the lower end of them stopping where the gulch began to widen into a long, high-country valley which ran east and west between the Shawmut Mountains on the south and the Aspen Rim on the north. Narrowing at its upper end, the gulch climbed and lost itself in the tumbled slope of Frosty Peak, where the source of Vining Creek lay. Down the whole length of the diggings the creek raced, foaming and brawling, full fed with icy water from the melting snow which still banked pure and white on Frosty Peak.

Along the flats and bars a horde of men toiled in a concentrated fever of gold hunger. Some squatted at the water's edge, jiggling and swirling gold pans interminably, scooping the final pinch of yellow residue from each panning into soggy buckskin pokes. Other men worked at crude rockers. Some were content merely to work the surface sand and gravel and earth, but there were many who burrowed like rodents in raw-earthed shaft holes, working down to bedrock, hoping to find a pocket there that would enrich them hugely and quickly. All were daubed with mud, soaked with water and sweat. It was a strange mixture of brute toil and feverish dreams. It was a placer diggings, booming and rich.

Jim Teague stood with Rupe Caldwell on a long, wide spreading sand and gravel bar. Here saws were whining and hammers pounding as a crew of men fashioned a

44

stretch of sluice box.

"We'll be ready to turn water into the sluices tomorrow," said Caldwell. "There'll be gold against the riffles of the boxes by tomorrow night. From then on, anything can happen. You go ahead and take a look around, Jim, so you'll have the lay of the land in your mind. I'll see you later."

Caldwell headed back to town and Teague sauntered casually along through the diggings. But when he left the long bars where the sluice box was going up, he ran into a rude surprise. A stocky, powerful miner with rippling black beard and fierce blue eyes was toiling at the handle of a creaking windlass set up over a shallow shaft. He had just brought up a wooden bucket of muddy gravel and piled it on a dump beside the shaft. Now he stepped over to one side and caught up a rifle, letting the muzzle of the weapon settle in a line with Teague's belt buckle.

"Far enough!" came the harsh growl. "You'll be turning around and heading out of here."

Teague looked at the miner levelly, the corners of his eyes pinching down. "Any law against a man taking a walk?" he drawled.

"As far as such as you walking on this claim, yes," came the blunt answer. The

45

miner patted the breech of his rifle. "This is the law."

"What have you got against me?" Teague asked. "I never saw you before."

The miner spat deliberately. "But I saw you. And with Rupe Caldwell. You're just another of his bully boys. So you'll not be snooping and spying around on any claim belonging to Barney Foxx and Dave Jordan. No, there'll be none of Caldwell's thievin', murderin' crew pushing me and Dave Jordan around. And you can tell Rupe Caldwell that Barney Foxx said that. Now be off!"

Jim Teague shrugged and turned away. Just another of those little men, he thought, knowing blind, stubborn animosity toward a bigger one. It was the old, old story. Move out ahead of the pack and you soon had them snarling and baying at your heels. Teague thought back to rough days on the open range. Even there, it was like Caldwell had said. Men battled for open range, and the one who won it was forever after a thief and a crook to those who lost out. Here, the only difference was that instead of open range, placer gold claims marked the prize. Yeah, this miner, Barney Foxx, was just another one of the yapping pack.

But within the next half hour Teague

found that there were many such. Not a single miner, laboring on his claim, gave Teague friendly greeting. All were surly, suspicious, and virtually all made some harsh and bitter reference to Rupe Caldwell and all of Caldwell's men and associates. Several of them let Teague see the business ends of guns.

Teague left the diggings completely, climbing up the low, running slope of the foothills west of town. A thin thread of cold anger was burning in him. He wasn't used to this sort of thing. Back in the saddle-and-cow country men didn't throw guns on Jim Teague and profanely order him off any trail he chose to cover, not with impunity. It might, he thought bleakly, be a good idea to give somebody a lesson in manners; put the fear of God into a couple of these surly fools.

This thought and the anger behind it soon burned away, however, before the disquieting realization that already, though he'd been in this placer camp of Bonanza Gulch considerably less than twenty-four hours, he was a marked man, and to most men, a distrusted and disliked one. Why? Because he had become identified with Rupe Caldwell. It was a sobering fact.

He moved slowly back to town, struck

again as he approached it by its rough-and-ready makeup, ugly and unplanned. Booming now, and to become more so with every stage and rumbling freight outfit coming in across the Shawmuts from Timber Lodge, yet there would always be an impermanence about it. Big as its present days were, those days were numbered. They were days that would continue only so long as the diggings yielded up gold. Once the diggings were worked out, this town would die, swiftly and completely. The west was full of remnants of such camps as this one. Ghost camps, dead and crumbling.

Out of this town's death a few men would emerge with a stake against the future. But most would leave as they had come, light of pocket and looking hungrily for a new gold-tinted rainbow to chase. Men came to Bonanza Gulch for one thing only. Gold! And all the fools would go away without any. . . .

Back in town and tobacco hungry, Teague headed for the trading post. He was still a little distance from it when Janet Sherrill stepped from its door, carrying a basket heaped with groceries and other supplies. She was bare of head, dressed in gingham and with a little wool jacket snugly buttoned against the crispness that was in the air despite the brightening play of spring sunshine. She made an appealing, domestic picture as she started angling across the street.

Two men moved out deliberately to intercept her. One was the dapper, cold-eyed killer, George Ides, The other was the gambler who had annoyed her on the stage and whom Teague had seen the evening before, dealing faro in the Big Nugget. The two, barring her way, made quite a show at politeness, doffing their hats. George Ides even reached out to relieve her of her heavily laden market basket, but the swiftness with which the girl drew back showed her feelings in the matter.

Jim Teague hurried his stride. As he closed in he heard Ides say glibly, "Introductions are in order, Miss Sherrill. Myself — George Ides. My friend — Ad Forsythe. We'll be happy to help you with that basket."

"I need no help, thank you," retorted the girl coldly, her chin high, the shine of indignation in her eyes. "Please get out of my way!"

"Couldn't think of it," said Ides smoothly. "That basket is much too heavy —"

Forsythe, the gambler, said something in a swift, low voice. Ides broke off his unctuous words, his head jerking up as he stared at Teague, who was now but a stride away.

The girl turned and, as she recognized Teague, exclaimed in swift relief.

"Mr. Teague!"

Teague touched his hat. "What is it, Miss Sherrill, a pair of mongrels in the way?"

She stammered a trifle. "These — these two — they —"

Teague nodded. "I understand." He looked at Ides and the gambler and his voice rang coldly. "Git!"

The gambler's glance went shifty and he started to edge away. George Ides did not move, except to straighten his shoulders. He had pale eyes which now took on a moiling blankness. His voice went almost whisper-thin. "Just a minute! Was that word — mongrels?"

"Mongrels it was," Teague rapped. "If the word rats suits you better — use it!"

The girl touched Teague's arm. "No!" she murmured. "Come away. There must be no trouble —"

"My dear young lady," cut in Ides, a droning mockery in his voice, "the trouble has already started. A loose mouth always starts trouble — trouble — !"

While he spoke, Ides' right hand had begun to steal up under his coat, toward his left armpit. Jim Teague's answering move was fast and utterly ruthless. He rolled forward on his toes, his right fist lashing out. It smashed into Ides' face, knocking the dapper gunman reeling back on his heels. Teague followed up on the blow, a cold, explosive roughness rushing out of him. For he had seen the gun that killed Jack Dorgan, the miner, come out of that same shoulder holster which George Ides carried.

Teague slashed the taut side of his left forearm against Ides' throat as the gunman tottered, head thrown back by the impact of that first savage punch. He caught at Ides' wrist with his right hand, yanking the arm down and back and across his bent knee with a wrenching power that wrung an involuntary gasp of agony from Ides and forced the man to drop his gun. Then Teague gave Ides a throw which sent him sprawling.

Teague scooped up Ides' gun and swung the muzzle toward Forsythe, the gambler, fully expecting that he would have to use it in the next split second. But Forsythe was making no move toward a weapon. Instead, his spread hands lifted slowly to shoulder height.

"I pass!" he mumbled.

Teague looked him up and down in scathing contempt. "Once a tinhorn, always a tinhorn!" That cold, explosive roughness was in Teague's voice as well as in his eyes.

"I told you once before that Miss Sherrill prefers to be left alone. This is the second time. I'll never tell you again — with words. On your way!"

Forsythe turned, hands still half-lifted, and went up the street. Teague looked at George Ides. The dapper gunman was trying to get to his feet. Already his mashed lips were puffed and grotesque and there was a trickle of crimson running down his chin. He rocked back and forth on his hands and knees groggily. When he did finally struggle erect he was gripping his wrenched right elbow and was choking thickly from that wicked, back-handed slash across the throat. For a moment he stared at Jim Teague, cold hell in his pale eyes. Then he turned and lurched away.

Teague watched Ides, captured gun in his hand, watched until Ides, his stride steadying as he went along, turned into the Big Nugget. With a killer like Ides, a smart man took no chances at all. When Ides disappeared, Teague dropped the gun into his coat pocket and turned to Janet Sherrill.

She was looking at him with wide, frightened eyes, her expression that of one who had just seen a person she thought she knew, turn into a stranger full of rough and crushing deadliness. It was like seeing a cold, but even breeze abruptly become a destroying, raging tempest.

Teague reached out, took the basket from her and said gruffly, "Come along. Now you know why you shouldn't be in a town like this."

She moved along beside him, her chin defiant, little spots of crimson burning in her cheeks. "I don't see why you should be cross at me. It wasn't my fault."

Teague glanced at her, some of the rough turmoil leaving his eyes. Even a hint of a smile tugged at the grimness of his lips. "Bless your heart, girl — I'm not cross at you. Your only fault is something you can't help."

"What is that?"

"Last night I heard a man put it just about right. He said you were pretty as a snow flower."

"Bosh! The man was daft. But even if it were true, is that a fault?"

"In a rough, tough camp like this, it's bound to be a cause of certain annoyances to you. Like today."

She considered this for a moment of silence, then asked, "Would you have me different?"

"No. But for my own peace of mind I

would have you somewhere else than in Bo-nanza Gulch."

She met Teague's glance, startled by words that could have meant more than they seemed to. Across their locked glances something swept, some strange, deep, shaking current. The girl looked away, coloring warmly.

"I'm glad," she said gravely, "that you're in Bonanza Gulch, Jim Teague. For it gives me a strange sense of security. Which doesn't quite make logic, does it? For we've known each other — how long? Not even a day. Yet, that is the way I feel."

They had come to the Sherrill cabin. Teague turned the basket of groceries over to her. "Your father?" he asked. "He's better?"

"Much. My biggest worry now is keeping him in bed. He wants to be up and about. He's all worked up over his claim, saying that some man named Caldwell is out to rob him. I wouldn't know anything about that, yet. I'm quite satisfied in knowing that Dad is going to be well again. Now, thanks once more. It seems," she ended, with a grave, level smile, "that I'm always thanking you for something."

"No thanks necessary," shrugged Teague. "I've already had my reward. Just seeing and speaking to you is enough."

Again their eyes locked and again that warm, strange, rushing current. Her smile softened. "I'll see you again, Jim Teague."

She went into the cabin and Teague turned back toward town. There was a man coming toward him. It was Les Jardeen and there was no friendliness in Jardeen's look at all. He said bluntly "I don't care to see you around this cabin again, Teague."

Teague looked him up and down, eyes chilling. "No? why?"

"You know why," Jardeen retorted. "You're one of Caldwell's crowd. So you're not wanted around here. Keep away."

Again Teague looked him up and down, noting the fair hair, the thinly handsome features, almost too much so, for that narrowness of face seemed to push Les Jardeen's eyes too close together. Teague nodded, as though he had seen something which interested him. He murmured, as though to himself, "I'll take a bronc with well-spaced eyes, every time. Friend, you're outsize for your boots. And you dance in the wrong places with the wrong kind. Don't try and get proud with me."

Abruptly Teague's glance was boring and harsh. Les Jardeen's eyes flickered, moved away. He turned and went into the cabin.

Teague stood for a moment, head slightly bent, a certain somberness sweeping his face. Then he pulled fully erect and walked away. The weight in his coat pocket reminded him of the gun he had taken away from George Ides. He brought it out to unload it — an instinctive thought and move. He stopped short, starting at the weapon.

This was not the orthodox gun of the frontier, the Peacemaker Colt, with a loading gate. This was not a solid frame gun. This weapon broke at the top. It was a .44 Russian model.

Teague's thoughts whipped back to the scene of the stage holdup on the road across the Shawmuts. To where two men lay dead near a treasure box that was looted and empty. Where a pair of saddle mounts had been tied and where he had found a freshly fired and discarded cartridge shell.

That shell had been a .44 Russian!

Jim Teague moved slowly, thinking of this.

Back in the door of the stage station, stout Ben App stood staring at a place in the street, now empty, where George Ides had rolled on his back, his mouth beaten and bloody. The chunky stage agent had seen it all, from the moment Janet Sherrill first stepped from the trading post to when she

56

and Jim Teague had moved away toward Duff Sherrill's cabin.

Ben App cast back over every detail and his eyes gleamed and he nodded with satisfaction. "I saw it," he murmured to himself. "I saw it all. I saw George Ides knocked into the dirt. I saw his gun taken away from him. I saw him handled like he was a puling infant instead of a damn cold-blooded killer that's had this camp buffaloed and walking around him in circles. Yes, sir — I saw all that!"

He grinned at nothing and thumped a pudgy fist into an open palm and announced to nobody and everybody. "There's a man arrived in this damned camp. By crickey, yes! A man — !"

III

GUN GUARD

The bartender in the Big Nugget who first saw George Ides enter thought the dapper gunman was drunk, for Ides weaved from side to side as he walked. In a way, Ides was drunk, drunk with a rage that numbed his brain and half-blinded him. There had always been a wicked cruelty in George Ides and there had always been a queer, almost perverted pride, too. He was like some jungle cat, ready to revert to the law of fang and claw at any time, but resenting a manhandling above all else. In his way, the man was fastidious. To have been knocked down, rolled in the dirt of the street, that was the greatest indignity in his twisted code. The man was writhing as though plunged in acid.

Ad Forsythe, the gambler, who had come into the Big Nugget just ahead of Ides, began a mumbled explanation of his own craven actions.

"You know, George — if I'd had any idea that guy —"

He broke off, gulping, stumbling back a

step, for the look Ides threw at him was a scorching, terrible thing, carrying more impact than a blow in the face. In that moment Ad Forsythe realized that if George Ides had still had his gun, he'd have used it on him. At this moment George Ides was all mad killer, rank with venom. Ad Forsythe kept on edging away, shaking with cold sweat.

Ides went on down the length of the bar, sliding a hand along it as though to steady himself. He circled the far end, went in behind it, grabbed a couple of bar towels, dabbed them with water and pressed them to his bleeding mouth. Then he turned and went into the side room.

Rupe Caldwell was in there, running over some account books. Slouched at length in another chair was Wade Riker, the sheriff. George Ides slammed the door behind him and stood there, mopping the blood from his chin. His head was dropped slightly forward and out of its half shadow his pale eyes burned almost sightlessly.

Rupe Caldwell, jarred by the slamming of the door, reared straight in his chair, angry words forming on his lips. But as he met the pale blaze in Ides' glance he went perfectly still for a long moment. Then words jerked out.

"Good God, George — what's the matter with you?"

Ides formed his reply slowly and the words came out of his tortured throat in a dragging hoarseness.

"He hit me. He knocked me into the mud. He may be a friend of yours, Rupe — but the next time I look at him it'll be over the sights of a gun. That man belongs to me! I want to see him kick."

"Who hit you?" asked Caldwell. "What man are you talking about?"

Ides seemed to gather himself, as though to launch a blow of some kind. But this was just the mad hate swelling in him. He let the words out in a gusty snarl.

"Teague! I'll start to live again when I see that fellow dead at my feet."

Rupe Caldwell used up a little time getting a stogie lighted. Then he pointed to a chair and said mildly, "Sit down, George. Relax, man. Now, what's this about Teague?"

"I told you. He hit me — knocked me down. I'll kill — !"

Caldwell broke in, roughly now. "Why did he manhandle you? He must have had a reason."

Caldwell's calculated harshness jerked Ides back to earth. "All right," said Caldwell

60

again, "why did Teague manhandle you?"

A shade of sullenness came into Ides' manner, pushing aside the blank fury. "We spoke to that girl of Sherrill's. Ad Forsythe and I did. The silly little fool was uppity as hell. About then Teague came along and got rough. Forsythe, the yellow whelp, backed down cold. Then Teague —" Ides shrugged, using the towels on his mouth again.

Wade Riker smiled thinly. "You showed damn poor judgment, George. Next time you'll know better than to step out of place."

Ides whirled on him. "Out of place?" he rapped hoarsely. "Why shouldn't I speak to that girl — ?"

"Because," cut in Riker drily, "she's the kind of girl she is, while you're the kind of man you are. Simple as that."

The blankness came into Ides' eyes again. "And what kind of a man am I? Listen, Riker, don't you ever try and —"

"That'll do, George," cut in Caldwell. "Wade, you keep out of this. But Wade's right, George — that was a fool play. You should have known better than that. No other one thing could turn this whole camp red-eyed and savage after all our scalps than to have one of our crowd annoy that girl. See that it don't happen again. About Teague, did you try and go for your gun?"

61

Ides nodded sullenly.

"Then," rapped Caldwell, "you were a double fool. You're lucky to be alive. Thought I told you about Teague."

"He's not that good," blurted Ides. "Another time —"

"Another time and you'll be dead. I've seen Teague work. He's poison. When I went to the trouble of getting him in here I did it because I knew I was buying poison. That man could give you a two jump lead on the draw and still beat you to it. In the future, remember that."

"So you're going to let him push the rest of us around, is that it?" demanded Ides. "The rest of us got to get off the trail when the great man comes along? Well, I don't. That's flat. I tell you, that man belongs to me."

Ides was steadying down and was all the more dangerous because of it. Caldwell saw this and adopted a more soothing manner. "I'll speak to Teague and let him know just how much weight he packs around here. But you cool off now, George. Use your head, man. You know what kind of a good thing we got here. We play this game right and we all go out of this camp rich men. If you got any grudges, save 'em until after we clean up. Then, if you figure you got anything to settle with Teague, fly to it. That will be your privilege — if you want it."

"I'll want it." Ides' voice was clearing now, his throat muscles beginning to loosen up. "I'll live for that day."

Ides went out, back into the barroom. Wade Riker said, "There's a man who can turn mad dog, Rupe."

Caldwell shrugged. "He's a valuable one just now. Let him lay."

Riker yawned and stretched and left, and presently Caldwell did the same, heading over to his cabin, where he found Jim Teague putting together a bite of midday food. Caldwell's smile was a trifle set.

"What's this I hear about you getting into a little trouble with George Ides and Ad Forsythe, Jim?"

"What did you hear?" asked Teague bluntly.

"Why, that you manhandled Ides and made Forsythe back down. And right out in the middle of the street where everybody could see. The story must have traveled far by this time and isn't going to do us any good."

"No? How is that?"

"Well, for one thing it gives the other side confidence if they see us fighting among ourselves. For another, it just isn't good policy to have ill feeling crop up among the boys working for me. If any fighting is to be done, I want it all directed where it will do the most good, which means — against the opposition."

Teague spooned some coffee into the pot. "You tell Ides and Forsythe that, Rupe?"

A flicker of annoyance showed in Caldwell's face at the bluntness of Teague's words and manner. "Yeah, I told them. Now I'm telling you."

Teague squared around and looked Caldwell straight in the eye. "I've traveled some pretty rough, tough trails in my time, Rupe, which have probably left me with my share of rough edges. I can stand a lot of things, but there is one thing I can't — and won't. And that is to see such as George Ides and Ad Forsythe annoying a decent woman. For your information there was no gun drawn except by George Ides. I took it away from him, rough. Did you expect me to stand there and let that cheap killer smoke me down? You ought to know me better than that. He's lucky I didn't kill him. If he ever tries to throw a gun on me again, I will kill him. You can tell him that for me."

There was a smoky darkness building up in Teague's gray eyes, which no man as shrewd as Rupe Caldwell could afford to ignore. Caldwell forced a return of that genial laugh.

"Pshaw! You take things too serious, Jim. George and Ad meant no harm. They just wanted to say hello to a pretty girl."

"If they told you that, they lied," rapped Teague harshly. "On the stage coming in I had to warn that tinhorn, Forsythe, to mind his manners toward Miss Sherrill. Neither he or Ides is fit to be in the same county with such as her."

Caldwell laughed again. "Same old Jim Teague. Once he gets his neck bowed he don't unkink easy. Well, do me a favor. Try and get along with the rest of my boys, will you?"

Teague shrugged. "That will be strictly up to them. But none of them want to try and throw a gun on me. Grub's ready. Drag up a chair."

Rupe Caldwell ate heartily. "This is plenty good," he declared. "Hashhouse grub gets tiresome after a time. This takes me back to the old times. How did things look to you along the diggings, Jim?"

"Mining is out of my line," admitted Teague. "I wouldn't know gold-bearing gravel from slide rock. One thing I did find out that I couldn't be mistaken about. You and everybody working for you are anything but popular around this camp, Rupe."

"Who loved Garr Paden, back along Wagon Wheel River, Jim? Nobody. That's the price the guy on top always has to pay. Don't let it worry you. Fifty ounces of gold a month can make up for a lot of dislikes, don't you think?"

"I'll survive," said Teague drily. "When do I start doing something to earn that fifty ounces?"

"Tonight. I'll leave the guard organization up to you. You can figure out your own shifts and run things your own way, just so you see to it that nobody does any fooling around my claims and sluice boxes who has no real business there. Soon as we finish eating I'll take you over to the other cabins and have you meet the boys."

There were three men in the first cabin and at Caldwell's summons they came out and followed him and Teague over to the third of these three cabins which stood together among themselves, and significantly apart from the rest of the town. Which was, mused Teague, indicative of the way things were shaping up as far as the general sentiment of Bonanza Gulch ran. Rupe Caldwell and his organization against the rest of the camp.

There were four men in the third cabin.

Two of these were the bullet-headed individual with the close-curling black hair and the hulking brute with the red hair and beard whom Teague had seen coming out of Caldwell's side room in the Big Nugget the previous night. Caldwell introduced the redhead as Bully Girard and the bullet-headed one as Curly Bolan. The other five were Case, Sharpe, Hamper, Burge and Tappan.

"Jim Teague is a long-time friend of mine, boys," explained Caldwell. "I punched cattle with him in the old days. I saw him fight a range war back on the Wagon Wheel River, so I know what he can do. You boys will take orders from him on this guard detail. Any questions?"

There seemed to be none. Teague said, "I'll figure out the shifts and let you know before evening."

When he and Teague went out, Caldwell asked, "What do you think of them?"

Teague shrugged. "Ask that when I know them a little better."

Down in the street there was a current of excitement flowing, centered in front of the trading post. Teague and Caldwell paused at the edge of the crowd there and listened to the talk of men swayed with gold fever. From bits of excited comment they pieced together what had happened.

Claus Lehrmann, whose claim was number four below Discovery, had sunk a shaft to bedrock and had hit a pocket. It was raw gold he'd taken out. One nugget as big as a walnut, others the size of peas. In less than four hours, so one miner claimed, the lucky man had taken better than eight thousand dollars out of that pocket. Another in the crowd claimed it was only five thousand. They would know for sure, soon. Claus Lehrmann was in the trading post now, having Joe Ruppert weigh up the find.

Jim Teague, rolling a cigarette, studied the faces of men in the crowd and found in all of them some shade of a common expression. It tightened their cheeks, put a flame in their eyes. Gold! The yellow metal around which men built fabulous dreams. The thing so many of them pursued as some sort of elusive will-o'-the-wisp, finding just enough to keep their dreams alive, so that they gave away the fat years of their lives in the chase, so that they toiled tremendously, suffered hardship and privation almost without limit and went finally to lonely graves, their last knowing vision still colored with the same consuming fever. Gold!

This thing had not touched Teague as yet. Hard-headed and practical, he knew full well the value of money and what it could do toward making a man's life full and content. Yet, as he viewed life, there were many things of great value that a man could savor that had no relation to gold at all. Small things, and most of them free.

Summer twilight, warm and blue and still, with birds cheeping sleepily in desert sage or in some willow thicket along a wilderness stream. Dawn thundering up across the rim of the world, giving a man a new day to look forward to, a new day to be greeted with the zest of robust health after a night of sound sleep had filled the spring of a man's well-being to overflowing. The smell of bacon in the pan and coffee in the pot when a man's hunger lay keen and biting within him. Cold, sweet water across a man's tongue when an aching thirst had him by the throat. These, too, were things to put a fine flavor in a man's life, and they had little, if any relation to gold.

The color of the stuff might drive some mad. But, mused Teague cynically, for him there would always be much more beauty in the sight of fat cattle grazing a wide, fat range. Gold was a dead, inanimate thing and the real gift of the world was the privilege of living.

Teague brought his glance to Rupe Caldwell and what he saw in Caldwell's face, made his glance still and fixed. For in the play of expression and the burn in his eyes, Caldwell betrayed a gold hunger as great as that of the most fervid miner in the crowd.

The crush about the door of the trading post gave back, letting out a brawny, jubilant young miner. His head was bare and his tousled hair was yellow as ripe wheat in the sunlight. His sea-blue eyes were shining and his broad, mud-streaked face exultant. He was carrying a heavy, water-darkened canvas poke and with both powerful hands pushed it high above his head. The word ran swiftly through the crowd. Between six and seven thousand dollars' worth of coarse gold!

Rupe Caldwell's eyes glinted and his jaw grew rigid. Then, abruptly aware of Teague's glance, he laughed and shrugged. "The stuff breeds a fever in a man, Jim. You build visions of all that the stuff can buy for you, and yet, it isn't so much that, as it is just the devilish wonder and lure of the gold itself. Well, now you see how it goes. Remember the old days? Forty a month and found. And here that big Dutchman digs himself a hole in the ground and comes up with thousands of dollars' worth of gold."

"And," retorted Teague drily, "he might dig a hundred more holes and not come up with even so much as a thin dime. Lot of luck in a deal like that, Rupe."

Over in the door of the stage station Ben App stood, a certain solid quality of character about his stocky figure. He had seen and heard all that went on, but right now his glance was fixed on Teague and Rupe Caldwell. Teague, happening to meet the glance, knew a stirring restlessness under it, for it was a look that held a mixture of grim appraisal and a certain regret. Jim Teague had the strange feeling that his worth had been weighed and that the balance came up short.

The first night on guard passed quietly. Jim Teague split his crew up into two shifts, the first from dark to midnight, the second from midnight to daylight. He headed the second shift himself, and with him took Burge, Tappan and Sharpe. He had put Case, a thick-shouldered, hard-jawed man, in charge of the first shift. He had picked Case because, while obviously a tough one, Case had a steady eye.

"No trouble?" asked Teague, when he took over from Case.

"Not from the outside," Case said. "But Bolan sneaked off on me for an hour. I made the rounds the way you said, every other

71

hour. Last time around, Bolan wasn't at his post. I waited for him and he didn't show up until about fifteen minutes before shift change."

"What did he have to say for himself?"

"Said he got cold and went uptown for a drink."

"I'll have a talk with him before he goes on shift again," promised Teague.

It was cold enough in all truth, down on the open gravel bars. The stars glittered with a frigid whiteness, letting down a pale light. The breath of Frosty Peak pressed in, carrying on it the bitter essence of altitude and of packed snowbanks. The physical presence of the peak was big and black against the stars.

Teague paced and smoked the hours away, drawing on a patience that was almost stoicism. This sort of thing took him back to nights on the open range when he had hawked bedded cattle herds, riding around them, singing to them. But those, he mused, were better nights, for the world was a milder place and the massed cattle gave off warm, bovine odors and a man had a greater sense of something real to guard, something warm and alive.

Here there was nothing but gravel crunching under his boot-heels and all sounds were caught up and smothered by the steady icy rush of the creek waters, and the breath of that was damp and penetrating.

Most of the town was already dark and silent when the midnight shift began, and Teague watched the rest of the lights go out, one by one. Those in the Big Nugget were the last to fade. After that there was just the grinding monotony of the small dead hours of the very early morning.

From time to time Teague checked his men, passed a word or two with them and understood the brief, profane surliness of their manner. Few men could be otherwise than sour, waiting out hours like these.

Dawn came in grayly, sharpening the loftier crests, pushing back the gulch shadows. The sluice box took gaunt shape, still dripping trapped water. The first scent of wood smoke brushed the nostrils. East, the sky began to warm up and glow. The last stars paled and faded out completely. Bonanza Gulch began to stir.

The sluicing crew came straggling down from town and Teague and his men turned things over to them. Teague went straight to Caldwell's cabin and turned in. He slept until noon. He shaved, had a good wash and cooked himself a meal. Then he went over to the other cabins, where he found Curly Bolan in the second one, taking his ease on a bunk. Bully Girard and some of the others were also in the place.

Curly Bolan sat up as Teague stood over him. "You'll be taking the second shift tonight, Bolan," Teague told him harshly. "And you'll stay on your post. I'll see to that."

"Why shouldn't a man go warm himself up with a drink?" argued Bolan. "No harm in that."

"You," pointed out Teague, "are supposed to help guard something. You don't do a job of it, lally-gagging uptown over a whiskey bottle. You can do your drinking before going on shift tonight, and that will have to last you. Now you know!"

A red spark glittered far back in Bolan's hard, black eyes. "Don't get oversize for your britches, Teague," he growled. "I know how much I have to take from you and how much I don't. And nobody pushes me around."

Jim Teague knew that right here he was being tested. The measure of his future authority over these men was to be settled at this moment. He acted with ruthless abruptness. He shot out a long arm, gathered in a handful of shirt front, jerked Bolan to his feet, shook him and threw him back on the bunk again. "You can," he rapped coldly, "learn the hard way if you want, Bolan!"

Curly Bolan reacted with the speed and deadliness of a snake. He bounced off the bunk and from somewhere, blindingly swift, snatched a knife. A man less alert than long training in violence had made Jim Teague, could never have avoided the wicked lunge of that naked steel. As it was, Teague barely moved clear.

The violence of Curly Bolan's lunge threw him off balance. Before he could recover, Teague drove a down chopping right fist, smashing home to the side of Bolan's neck just under the ear. The impact was sodden, and dropped Bolan to his hands and knees, half-stunned. The knife, carried forward and down as Bolan fell, drove deep into the puncheon floor of the cabin and stuck there, quivering.

Teague locked his left hand in Bolan's collar, hauled him to his feet, squared him around and hit him again, getting the full roll of his shoulder behind this one. The punch dropped Bolan in a senseless sprawl across his bunk. Teague kicked the knife under the bunk and turned to face the others in the room.

Only one of them had made an antagonistic move. Bully Girard reared up on the edge of his bunk and poised there, not unlike some hulking, rusty-maned animal about to spring. His eyes were red rimmed and wicked.

Teague hooked a thumb in his belt, looked Girard over coldly. "Something you wanted to say, Girard?"

Girard snarled soundlessly, but nothing more. Teague turned and left the cabin. Girard began to curse, blisteringly. Jack Case, the hard-jawed one, spoke bluntly.

"Stow it, Girard! If you meant to eat fire, you had your chance. But you cooled off quick when Teague was looking at you. Don't try and fool yourself. That was a tough man who just left this cabin — a damn tough one. He made a monkey of George Ides and you just saw how he handled Bolan. Me, I say Jim Teague is a good man to leave alone!"

On leaving the cabin, Teague headed down for the diggings. A stage, just in from Timber Lodge, pulled up in front of Ben App's stage station and began unloading. Word spread quickly along the street that several sacks of mail had come in on the stage and that Ben App would have it sorted and ready to distribute within an hour. Men hurried to spread these glad tidings all through town and across the creek flats.

Down on Discovery, water was rushing and splashing through the long sluice boxes, pouring out of the lower end in a muddy torrent. Men were toiling, shoveling more and more of the gold-bearing sands and earth into the boxes, where the restless water tore at it, broke it up and washed it away, the heavier particles of gold dropping down to be caught and held behind the riffle cleats.

Rupe Caldwell was there, moving up and down beside the sluices. As Teague came up to him, Caldwell plunged a hand into the turbulent sluice, brought out a pinch of sediment from behind a riffle. He put this on the palm of his other hand, spread it around with a forefinger. "Look, Jim," he invited.

The sediment was shot through with flecks of gold. "More of that going into the sluices with every shovelful," announced Caldwell exultantly. "Rich — rich as hell! Now you know why you got an important job on your hands guarding these sluices."

"Maybe you could stand a better breed of men for the job, Rupe," said Teague briefly. "One in particular. Curly Bolan sneaked out on us last night. Claimed he got cold and went uptown for a drink. When I called him about it a few minutes ago he tried to get tough on me. I handled him pretty rough."

Caldwell's eyes flickered. "How rough?"

"He pulled a knife on me. I slapped him down. He'll live. But," added Teague, the old harshness creeping into his tone, "if he ever reaches for that knife again on me, I'll finish him. You better make it damn plain to all your crowd, Rupe, that I don't stand for that sort of business. George Ides tried for his gun, Bolan for a knife. I'm through using my fists. If I'm to boss your guard crew, then they'll do as they're told and no back talk. Otherwise somebody is really going to be hurt."

Caldwell nodded slowly. "I'll make it plain to them. Curly Bolan isn't a bad sort. But he's got a hair-trigger temper. I may take him off the guard job entirely and give you a new man. Say — what's the attraction uptown? First time I've seen so many pulling away from the diggings at this time of day."

Caldwell waved an arm toward a number of miners who were hurrying up out of the flats.

"Stage just came in, with mail," Teague explained.

"Well, now — I'm expecting some mail myself," said Caldwell. "Let's get up there."

As they climbed toward town, Teague and Caldwell passed not far from the Sherrill cabin. A gaunt and grizzled man, obviously not long from a sick bed, was moving slowly around in front of the cabin in the crisp sunshine. To steady himself he had a rude, homemade cane in one hand, while his other hand rested on the slim, erect shoulder of Janet Sherrill.

It seemed to Jim Teague that even at this distance he could see this gaunt man's sunken eyes flash with anger. And across that distance came the man's voice, hollow with weakness, yet with a certain deeply booming resonance.

"I'm coming back, Caldwell. Your knifeman wasn't quite clever enough to make the job on me complete. Yeah, I'm coming back. It won't be long now. And then we'll see, Caldwell. You're due to find that honest law hasn't forgotten the decent men in this camp. Things will be on the move before long. I'll see to that. And then there'll be a noose waiting for you, Caldwell — for you and everyone of your crooked whelps!"

Caldwell did not answer. Jim Teague touched his hat to Janet Sherrill, but got not the slightest hint of answering response. She looked at him, but she also looked through and past him, as though he were something that did not exist. Her face was pale and her head was high.

As they moved beyond earshot, Caldwell laughed. "Something familiar about that tune don't you think, Jim? Remember the yelps that went up against Garr Paden back along the Wagon Wheel River? The old loser's cry. Everybody is a crook except them. They were the only honest men."

Teague did not answer right way. Then he murmured, "That was Duff Sherrill, of course?"

Caldwell nodded. "Duff Sherrill. He gets in a drunken gambling brawl and somebody sticks a knife in him. So it is all my fault, of course. Everything that goes wrong in this camp is my fault, according to some of those moaning fools. Well, that's the way it goes. You beat them at their own game and they start throwing rocks."

There was a thickening crowd at the stage station. As Rupe Caldwell and Jim Teague pushed in among them, more than one antagonistic growl lifted, and Teague felt the impact of many hostile eyes. An instinctive cold prickling ran up his spine. Here was a group hatred that could turn into mob madness at any time.

To Caldwell, his voice tersely low, Teague said, "Better slide out of here, Rupe. This crowd could easily start throwing something worse than rocks. If there's any mail for you, I'll pick it up."

Caldwell's lips pulled back from his teeth a little. "Let 'em growl, Jim. They won't bite. It takes a leader to get fools like these started, and nobody wants to take the lead, against me. To hell with them!"

Teague studied Caldwell narrowly from the side, increasingly aware of things about the man that had not been there in the old days. Rupe Caldwell had never been exactly the shrinking violet type, but there had been a certain almost carefree geniality to the man which had made him likable and easy to be around. Now, however, there was an arrogance, a swagger, the hard-bitten defiance of a man utterly sure of himself and his own power; plus a ruthless disregard for everything and everyone standing in his way.

Ben App appeared at the door of the stage station, a bundle of mail stacked on one arm. He began calling off names and men with the weight of long months of loneliness riding them, pushed eagerly forward to receive precious reminders of home and the gentler side of life.

The stage agent had sorted the mail into

81

alphabetical order and soon he came to a letter which he looked at with narrowing eyes for a moment before calling the name. Then his head came up and he looked across the crowd at Jim Teague and Rupe Caldwell.

"For you, Caldwell," he said coldly.

Caldwell stepped forward to receive his letter. A growl ran through the crowd. A miner said, "Why waste time on such as him, Ben? Get on with the boys who count."

"The mail," pointed out Ben App tersely, "plays no favorites." Then he began calling out more names.

Caldwell came back to Teague's side, slipping his letter into the pocket of his coat. His lips were twisted sardonically. "Them who yelp loudest for what they call justice, are the first who'd deny it to others," he murmured.

Most of the names Ben App called out, found response, but to some names there were no answers and these letters the stage agent put carefully aside. He came to another name that brought no response and he called it out again.

"Claus Lehrmann! Where are you, Claus? Here's that letter you've been waiting for so anxiously. It's fat and heavy and the lady who wrote it has a fine and graceful hand.

Claus Lehrmann! —"

"Save it, Ben," advised a miner. "I reckon Claus is too busy taking another five or six thousand out of that pocket he struck to think about mail. Yeah, Claus will soon be ready to head back to the lady who wrote that letter, a rich man."

Another miner, mud-smeared and panting from hard running, came hurrying in from the diggings. He was unnoticed until he began pushing and burrowing through the crowd. Then men turned on him, annoyed and swearing at his thrusting insistence.

"Easy does it, pardner — easy!" came the word. "Your turn will come. If there's any mail for you, it'll keep."

The miner paid no heed, shoving and pressing forward until he broke out beside Ben App, who was just lifting his voice in a final call.

"Claus Lehrmann!"

"Claus won't be here, Ben," gulped the newly arrived miner. "Claus won't ever be here. He's dead, Ben!"

The miner's voice had carried clear, so now, instantly the crowd went completely still, the silence hanging like a suspended shadow in the air. Ben App finally broke it.

"Dead! You mean — Claus Lehrmann? How do you know?"

"Well, Claus is layin' in his tent down on his claim right now, knifed to death. I went over to tell him about the mail comin' in'. I thought he'd be workin' in his shaft. He wasn't, so I looked in his tent. There he was, half in and half out of his blankets. He's dead, all right." The miner's voice went a little husky. Then he added a final remark. "I liked Claus. He was a damn fine man."

Taut and alert, Jim Teague saw the dark wave of feeling that passed over Ben App's face. The stage agent's voice came out with eruptive harshness.

"How about his poke? What about that fat poke of raw gold he'd taken from that pocket — ?"

"Gone," shrugged the miner. "Leastways I didn't see nothin' of it around the tent. Of course I didn't do no searchin'. I come away from there fast, to spread the word. To me, it looked like whoever killed him mighta done it last night while he was sleepin', and that they'd rolled him half outa his blankets, like they mighta been searchin' for that poke. Mebbe they found it."

Something went over the crowd like a drift of bleak and icy wind. A mutter that was almost a snarl began and grew. Jim Teague took hold of Rupe Caldwell's arm and with sudden, steely strength began drawing him away. They were clear and moving upstreet before what Teague feared would come, did come. A sudden, furious yell bursting from a miner's throat.

"Where's Rupe Caldwell? Maybe Caldwell could give us an answer to all this. Him or one of them damn jack-legs workin' for him. Where's Caldwell? He was here just a minute ago!"

Teague pushed Caldwell around the corner of the trading post. "Get out of sight and stay out of sight, Rupe! This is dynamite, with a short fuse."

"The damned fools!" raged Caldwell. "I didn't kill that Dutchman. This is as much news to me as it is to anyone else."

"Maybe so," rapped Teague. "But they could hang you before you could prove it. You've made yourself a big man around this camp — maybe too big. And this is the sort of price you have to pay for that. Hurry up — get on out of sight! I'll see you later."

The crowd was milling around uncertainly, but lifting a common cry. "Where's Caldwell?"

For another short moment Caldwell listened to that cry, a hard, twisted defiance pulling tautly at his florid cheeks. Then he shrugged. "All right, Jim. I'll be at the Big Nugget."

Rupe Caldwell hurried off, dodging around the back of the trading past, circling wide for the sanctuary of his saloon and gambling hell. Jim Teague moved back to the street, a strange and brooding look chilling his face to bleakness. He watched the crowd mill and shift and saw that for this moment at least, it wasn't going anywhere. The temper was there, but not the plan. Just now the crowd had no definite leader to offer the plan and jell that temper. But should such a leader appear, there was no telling what might happen. For the shadow of Judge Lynch was in the air, grisly and ominous. . . .

IV

NIGHT RAID

Bonanza Gulch had quieted again. The first furious anger that had burned through the camp, as the word of Claus Lehrmann's murder spread, had, like any other too furious a flame, burned itself out. Men, intrinsically selfish, and with the lure of the diggings calling, had gone back to their claims, intent once more on their search for the yellow metal. Yet that flame had left another glowing ember in the minds and hearts of men, along with several others of its kind. Given time, leadership and the proper moment and incident, those gathering coals could break into an all-consuming conflagration of fury. There had been a tension in this town which Jim Teague had sensed the moment he arrived. That tension had increased twice over in the space of a day or two.

Sitting in the side room of the Big Nugget, Jim Teague warned Rupe Caldwell of this. "I don't know all the answers to what took place here in Bonanza Gulch before I came," said Teague. "And I don't know all the answers to what has happened since I arrived. But one thing I do know, Rupe. That is — you better be careful."

Caldwell studied him with narrowed eyes. "What do you mean — be careful? You're not suggesting that I had anything to do with the killing of that Dutchman, are you?"

Teague shrugged. "I'm suggesting nothing. I'm only saying what I know. Which is that this camp is ripe to explode. From all the signs that explosion could take place right under you. Yeah, you better go slow."

"Go slow — how?"

"Keep out of sight. Leave the running of your affairs to others. None of your crowd is popular in this camp, me included. But so far the miners seem satisfied to give us a growl and a curse and let it go at that. But you, you're like a red flag to a bull, Rupe. You set 'em off. Flatly, you'll be a fool if you don't quit pushing your luck so hard."

Caldwell swung an arm in a violent, contemptuous gesture. "Let 'em growl — let 'em talk! I tell you, Jim — it's the same old story, like it was against Garr Paden, back on the Wagon Wheel River. The losers yapping at the winners. That's all it will ever be, just yapping."

Teague spun a cigarette into shape, lighted it and inhaled deeply. "Something I never got around to tell you, Rupe. You keep going back to Garr Paden and how he played the game on the cattle range. Well, I was in Timber Lodge when your letter caught up with me. Ever stop to wonder why I was in Timber Lodge instead of still ridin' for Garr Paden?"

Caldwell laughed. "Probably because you got tired of doing the rough work for Paden for forty a month and decided to look for greener pastures."

"Wrong!" rapped Teague. "I was in Timber Lodge because Garr Paden's outfit wasn't an outfit any more. It was all through — busted up. And why? Because Garr Paden was dead. A dry-gulcher got him one night as he stood in the doorway of his own ranchhouse. Garr was a big man, boss of the range, up until that bullet hit him. Then he was nothing. A man who ends up with a rope around his neck is just the same. No matter how big he was before, when you cut him down you just got a bundle of clothes — and something to bury."

The confident, scoffing half smile on Rupe Caldwell's face became a little set. He got to his feet and took a short turn up and down the room. Teague saw that at last Caldwell was shaken.

"Damn it, Jim," Caldwell burst out, "you

give a man the creeps, talking like that. So Garr Paden is dead, after all. Well, he was a fool for ever standing in that lighted doorway."

"Maybe," agreed Teague thinly, "but more of a fool because he got to thinking himself so big and powerful the little fellow couldn't touch him. That's always a mistake and one you'd better not make, Rupe."

Caldwell came back to the table and sat down. There was a bottle and glasses there and he poured himself a stiff jolt. "Maybe you're right," he admitted. "I'll stay out of sight for a while. But that's going to be tough, for I've got much to do. That letter I received? Well, it was from a friend advising me of trouble ahead."

"What kind of trouble?"

"Legal trouble. That Sherrill girl you befriended, she brought the trouble in with her. An injunction calling on me to cease and desist all workings of number one below Discovery until the title to the claim has been thrashed out and settled in court."

"I thought," murmured Teague, "you said the law was on your side."

Caldwell spread his hands. "The law is like that. Some of it rules for one side, some for the other. I explained to you that the law demands that a man, on registering his claim, locate it physically within a reasonable exactness. And that if he does not, then the ground is open to claim by someone else. I've told you how much in error the locations of number one above and number one below Discovery were. The law is definitely with me in the relocation of those claims. This injunction, well, it doesn't mean a thing unless it is served on me by the proper, qualified authority. Which in this case would mean Sheriff Wade Riker. And," ended Caldwell, his sardonic smile coming back, "I don't think Riker will find time for that little chore."

Jim Teague took a final drag on his cigarette, then slowly ground the butt to pieces in his fingers. A vague shadow of distaste formed in his eyes, turning them wintry and bleak.

"I don't like that sort of thing, Rupe. I realize that this is a rough, tough, catch-as-catch-can sort of camp, with every man pretty much for himself. But there are limits and I got mine. Number one below Discovery — that was originally Duff Sherrill's claim, wasn't it? So, when you push Duff Sherrill around, you're doing the same to his daughter, Janet. And that I won't stand for. This is a pretty good time to make myself quite clear on that."

Rupe Caldwell lay back in his chair, the

heavy jolt of whiskey he had taken deepening the floridness of his cheeks. That face wasn't as firm as it had once been, decided Teague. There was a suggestion of a certain beefiness beginning to show about the jaw and a puffiness about the eyes. Rupe Caldwell had been too long away from a saddle, had spent too much time in this side room with a whiskey bottle. Physically, this man had softened up. But his eyes now carried a brittle shine.

"Well, now," he said with some harshness, "this is also a good time to get something else clear. You're working for me. Do as you're told and we'll get along fine. And you'll go out of this camp with more money in your jeans than you'd earn in a lifetime of riding for wages. But, Jim — don't try and tell me what I can or can't do. You just don't rate that big!"

"It's not a question of how big I am," retorted Teague. "The point is that you're not big enough to play the law both ends against the middle. I told you before that I had some conscience left. I find I got more than I thought. I'll still take my chances in a rough-and-tumble fight where it's an even break for every man. But I never could stand for a stacked deck. I've seen and heard things since I hit this camp that don't set well with me at all. Right now I'm wondering if you gave me a true picture of things the day I showed up here."

Their glances met and locked and it was Caldwell who looked away. He forced a laugh, but the old-time geniality was flat. He straightened up and slapped the table. "What the devil! We got no quarrel, Jim — you and me. We're acting like damn fools. I need you and you need me. There's a way out of this that'll satisfy both of us. I'll think on it."

"Fair enough," was Teague's laconic rejoinder. "But what I said stands. Janet Sherrill is not to be hurt in any way. I mean — any way! I'll see you later."

Teague left the Big Nugget and went along the street in shadowed thought. The gauntness that had been on him when he first came to Bonanza Gulch was already beginning to leave him. Food and sleep and activity in the open air were at work, rebuilding swiftly out of the deep spring of tough fiber that had always been part of him. His side gave him no trouble at all except an occasional twinge. Strength and well-being were running an ever-quickening tide through him.

The afternoon was getting along. A man came cutting across the street to intercept

Teague. It was Jack Case, of the guard crew. From the very first, Jim Teague had recognized in Jack Case a hard and solitary toughness, but also a certain worthiness, for this man quailed before the glance of no other man. Teague stopped.

"Something on your mind, Case?"

Jack Case nodded. "Been wanting a chance to talk to you. You heard about the murder of that miner, Claus Lehrmann?"

"Yeah," said Teague. "I heard. What about it?"

"Lehrmann," said Case quietly, "was killed some time last night — knifed to death in his blankets. Now then, there's an hour of disappearance last night which Curly Bolan can't account for except by claiming he left his guard post to go uptown for a drink. And Bolan is partial to knife work — in the back or in the dark, maybe. So, I can't help thinking and wondering, Teague."

"True," agreed Teague. "All of it. But what can be proven?"

Case shrugged. "Not a thing, but that ain't what I got in mind, even though the whole thing ties in so smooth I can't help but guess — while admitting I could be guessing wrong. After all, who knows what is really in the mind of any man in this

94

camp? Lots of men will do lots of things for gold. But the main point I'm driving at is this. I hired out to Caldwell to help guard some claims. That's right, ain't it?"

"That's the picture as I understand it," nodded Teague.

"All right. Those claims wouldn't have to be guarded if there wasn't some sort of ruckus going on as to who really owns them. I'm not worrying my head at all about that. I'm working for Caldwell now, but I could have been working for the other side if they'd propositioned me first. For all I know, maybe both sides are wrong, but I'm not worrying about that angle either. Teague, I just damn well don't like knife work and robbery in the dark. There's a hell of a difference between men fighting an honest row out in the open, and some low whelp with a knife slithering around in the dark and using that knife on some poor helpless devil while he's sleeping. No, sir — I don't like that!"

"Keno!" drawled Teague. "I don't like it either, Case. And I admit I was thinking along the same line you are when you came along. If I had to make a guess, it would be the same one you'd make. But it would still be only a guess, as you say. We can't prove a thing."

"Just for the hell of it, suppose we could prove something?" Case's jaw was outthrust, his eyes level. "What would your stand be, Teague?"

"I'd recommend a noose and the nearest tree," replied Teague bleakly.

Case said, "That makes two of us. I see I had you figured right. You and me look at things alike. So now I'll string along with the job for a while. But I want no part of that fellow Bolan around me. He so much as looks at me slant-eyed and I'll fix him and his dirty knife — quick!" Then, a hard smile crinkling his eyes slightly, Case added, "Right now Mister Bolan is a pretty subdued hombre. You didn't hold back none when you hit him, did you?"

Jim Teague came back up from the diggings under a sky spangled with chill, crystal-sharp stars. He had just seen to the placing of the first guard shift. Curly Bolan was not there, but Rupe Caldwell had sent another man, named Moulton, to take Bolan's place. And Jack Case, as before, was in charge of the shift.

There was a light gleaming ruddily in the Sherrill cabin and Teague, as he passed, almost unconsciously angled closer to the place. He stopped abruptly, however, as movement came past the front corner of the cabin, movement that resolved itself into two people, walking arm in arm.

They came just a little way, then walked back the same way they had come. Two people, sauntering under the stars. Teague heard their voices, identified them. Janet Sherrill and Les Jardeen.

Teague melted away into the dark, his eyes going somber. He ended up at the Big Nugget, idling through the crowd in the place. He thought, somewhat cynically, of the vagaries and inconsistencies of human thought and nature. He had seen plenty of evidence since coming to Bonanza Gulch, that the majority of the miners had little use for Rupe Caldwell. Yet, here they crowded the Big Nugget which Caldwell owned, spent their hard-earned dust across the bar, or lost it across the poker tables and at the faro layout. They squandered it on the dance hall girls and Caldwell grew richer by the minute. This they were doing tonight. Tomorrow they might very well be yelling for a rope and a tree to hang Caldwell to.

Teague saw that Ad Forsythe, the tinhorn, was again dealing at the faro layout, with George Ides again the lookout. Ides was as dapper as ever in his dress but the marks of Teague's fist still stood out in dark bruises on his face and Ides' lips were still puffed and swollen. Teague bought a cigar at the bar, lit it, took a chair against a wall and settled back to kill time until midnight, when he would go on guard shift again, down at Discovery.

Les Jardeen came in, had a drink at the bar, drifted from one gambling table to another to watch the play going on, and finally ended up at the rear of the place when the piano was beating out its rhythm and the dancers were whirling, the girls already bored and weary, the miners stamping and shuffling heavily. He did not see Teague, back against that shadowy wall.

Presently, into the beat of the music came those occasional jangling discords and Teague, swinging his head, saw that Les Jardeen was dancing again with that slim, dark-eyed girl. And the ugly little man at the piano would twist his head and watch them, every time they circled past, his eyes glittering.

After a bit the dance ended and Les Jardeen came back up through the gambling space once more, worked his way to the door and left the place. Then it was the dark-eyed girl he'd been dancing with who left the dance floor and circled to the door of Rupe Caldwell's side room. She knocked and went in.

Within a couple of minutes she came out again and went back to the dance floor. On her way she paused momentarily at the faro layout, close to George Ides. She apparently passed some remark to him, for Ides glanced at her and nodded. Shortly after, Ides slid down from the high lookout's stool, stepped over to a poker table and tapped another house man on the shoulder. The houseman tossed in his poker hand and took over the faro lookout's stool. Ides then went into Caldwell's side room.

It had all been casual and commonplace enough, of no meaning at all unless one had followed the entire sequence, which Jim Teague had, with brooding thoughtful eyes, because in the first place he'd been watching Les Jardeen. Yet these maneuverings brought no answer, held no meaning. Teague shook himself somewhat angrily. Perhaps he'd been imagining things, brought on by simmering suspicions and the resentment he felt toward Jardeen, resentment because Jardeen would one moment walk under the stars with a girl like Janet Sherrill, and then come into a dive like the Big Nugget and dance with one of the dance hall bevy.

Teague's cigar went out and the cold taste of it lay sour along his tongue. He ground the butt underfoot, got up and shouldered his way out into the night, heading for the diggings, even though he was not due to take over there for another two hours. But a vast restlessness was upon him, a biting unease within him that had begun as just the vaguest of stirrings, but which was now an endless tumult.

He had the feeling that he was being slowly enmeshed in the coils of a viciousness, a hypocrisy that was as murderous and unprincipled as it was cynical. Aside from the camp's plain dislike and distrust of Rupe Caldwell and all his doings, there wasn't a single thing Teague could point to and say flatly, "This is so." He could guess, he could surmise and reach fairly logical answers. But in all of these the last vital germ of complete proof was lacking.

As he walked along, one conviction came sweeping in out of the troubled tangle in his mind. It was that he could not go on acting one thing, thinking another. There was a decision in front of him and he had to make it, one way or the other. Either he must pull completely away from Rupe Caldwell and take the first stage out of Bonanza Gulch, or he must, once and for all, fully accept Caldwell and all his doings, doubt nothing and move with the tide. He couldn't be half one thing, half something else. Well, he'd have a good chance to think things out, once and for all, tonight in the silence and solitude of his guard shift. By tomorrow he'd know the answer.

He felt immediately better after coming to this decision. Recklessness poured through him and he felt the better for it. It was like a clean, strong breeze dissipating a cloying, choking mist. In his heart was a whisper of what his choice would be.

There was a light still burning in the Sherrill cabin and in abrupt impulse Teague went over to the door and knocked. A murmur of voices quieted inside and then it was Janet Sherrill who opened the door. The light from within fell fully on Teague and he heard the girl catch her breath slightly. She stiffened and said, "There must be some mistake. Aren't you calling at the wrong place?"

"No mistake," said Teague quietly. "I want to talk to you and your father. I hope you're alone."

"Who is it, child?" came Duff Sherrill's deep voice. "And what does he want?"

The girl hesitated slightly. "It — it's Mr. Teague. And he says he wants to talk with you and me, Dad."

"Teague! Why, ain't he the fellow that Les Jardeen says is one of Rupe Caldwell's right-hand men? Tell him to be off. No Caldwell man comes into this cabin. The gall of him!"

Janet Sherrill started to close the door. "You see," she said quietly.

"No!" Teague put out a hand, pushed the door back. He stepped into the cabin, swung the door closed and put his back to it. "No!" he said again. "You got to listen to me."

He heard a gun lock click and he looked across into the muzzle of the revolver which Duff Sherrill held, steady and menacing. The grizzled miner growled, "Get out! I'll shoot you in your tracks if you don't. I want no damned Caldwell spy prowling in my cabin. Get out, I say!"

Teague stared into the old miner's angry eyes and saw that he meant every word of his threat. "So you'd shoot me and the camp would probably say well done. And if that would prove anything, you tell me what it is. It'll pay you to listen to what I have to say, Sherrill. It won't take long."

"You must have a gun on you," rumbled Sherrill. "Go for it, so I can get this thing done!" He made a little stabbing motion with his weapon, but the girl cried softly, "No — Dad! Wait. It won't cost anything to hear him out. Let me handle this."

Duff Sherrill's gun lowered, but only

slightly. "I can think of nothing a Caldwell man can say to me that interests me. But, if you wish it that way, Janet — all right. Only, tell him to be quick about it."

She faced Teague, very erect, looking at him accusingly. "You understand that I share my father's sentiments fully. But for the sake of a kindness or two that you've done me, well — we're listening."

Teague inclined his head gravely. "You brought an injunction in with you from Timber Lodge, which calls on Rupe Caldwell to cease all work on a certain disputed claim until proper title to that claim has been settled by court authority. Isn't that so?"

It was plain that both of the Sherrills were startled by Teague's information. "I — I don't know how you could have learned of that," stammered the girl. "But admitting there is such an injunction — what about it?"

"To mean anything, it must be served by some accepted representative of the law. In this case, who would that be?"

"Why, Sheriff Riker, of course. I intend to give it to him in the morning and tell him to serve it."

"I wouldn't do that if I were you, Miss Sherrill."

Duff Sherrill's growl rang through the cabin. "What is that, a threat?"

"No. Just well-meant advice."

"Advice from a Caldwell man," scoffed Sherrill. "So that Rupe Caldwell could have more time to strip my claim with his damn sluice boxes. You must take me for the biggest fool unhung!"

"You'll be a fool if you ever let Riker get his hands on that injunction," said Teague levelly, "for he'd never serve it and you'd probably never see it again."

"He'll serve it," declared Duff Sherrill. "He'll have to. He's got no other out. So now you can go back to your boss, Mister Rupe Caldwell, and tell him he'll have to think up a better scheme."

It was plain to Teague that he could get nowhere trying to reason with this grizzled, embittered miner. He turned to the girl again. She seemed to read his thought, for she shook her head before he could speak.

"No, I won't try and persuade Dad to do differently. He has suffered a great deal at the hands of Rupe Caldwell and Caldwell's men. And I share his distrust of them, fully." There was a barrier in her eyes that had not been there during the first day or two of their acquaintance. "There is nothing more to be said."

Teague shrugged and turned away. "Very well. Sorry I bothered you."

The door closed behind him and he moved off into the dark. At first a bleak anger bit at him, but this soon faded in front of stark reasoning. He really couldn't blame the Sherrills for throwing his well-meant advice back in his teeth. After all, he was a Caldwell man and they had every reason to distrust and despise him as such.

But couldn't they see that Sheriff Wade Riker was a Caldwell man, too? Riker hung out a great part of the time in the Big Nugget, was in and out of Caldwell's side room regularly, which anyone could note if they looked around at all. It must, Teague decided, be the star that Riker wore. People got into a groove of thinking and accepted custom. To so many of them that star meant law and its authority, and they could not bring themselves to believe that it meant anything other than unbiased authority. They blindly refused to believe that the law could be perverted and that many men carried the star who were, in reality, scoundrels of the first water.

Well, he'd done the best he could in this matter. He'd betrayed Rupe Caldwell's confidence, and to no end. It was, Teague realized, the first time in his life that he hadn't been true to his hire, good or bad. And the thought made him squirm a trifle. For there was in him a streak of deep and fundamental honesty. He had traveled some pretty rough trails in his life, but always he had chosen one or the other and then stuck to that side, for better or for worse.

He told himself savagely that he'd have to make up his mind fully in this matter, one way or the other, and do it quick. Either he must be for Rupe Caldwell, or against him. There could be no half this and half that. He couldn't straddle. Else he'd lose his self-respect completely.

He owed it to Rupe Caldwell that he was now warmly clad and full fed, that he had money in his pocket and a warm, dry bunk to sleep in at nights. He had a job. All these things he could thank Rupe Caldwell for. But what else?

Caldwell had sold him a shoddy piece of goods. There was no use in trying to tell himself different, knowing now what he did. Caldwell had not given him the whole truth, nor any small part of it in his first explanation of the setup here in Bonanza Gulch. The battle over disputed gold claims was one thing and the right or wrong of that angle was something Teague had no answer for. But then there were the men Caldwell had surrounded himself with, who were his confidants. George Ides, Curly Bolan, Bully Girard.

Now there were three fine human buzzards. Not one of them was the kind that any man possessed of even a grain of honesty would have around him. And if Rupe Caldwell kept them working for him, then it must be because he had turned as lawless and unprincipled as they.

This was bitter stuff for a man to chew on. Teague was bleak and harsh when he went down to the diggings.

At midnight Jack Case and his crew of Moulton, Bully Girard and Hamper went off shift. Case reported all quiet. So then Jim Teague and his group of Tappan, Sharpe and Burge took over. At his post Teague squatted on his heels, coat collar turned up against the night's chill. He smoked one cigarette after another, still wrestling with his problem.

All things pointed to a replica of the previous night. Town was dark, all except the Big Nugget, where active life still hung on. A small, biting wind came drifting down from the humped-up blackness of the Shawmuts and it carried with it now and then the faint tumping of the Big Nugget's piano. But finally this sound ceased, the Big Nugget went fully dark and then the night's stillness was complete except for the rush and washing gurgle of creek waters and once, the far-off lonely mourning of a timber wolf's hoarse night song somewhere in the Shawmuts.

One of early morning's small cold hours drifted by. Then, off to his left, Teague heard Burge call a hard challenge. Teague was instantly on his feet, staring through the dark, then moving swiftly toward Burge. He sent a low call ahead of him and Burge answered.

"What was it?" Teague asked as he came up.

"Boots shuffling on gravel," Burge told him. "Yonder, toward the head of the sluice box."

"Maybe some miners, late from town, heading for their tents on their claims," suggested Teague.

"Maybe," Burge growled. "There was more than one. Sounded like a bunch of them."

"We'll take a look around," said Teague, leading the way,

They worked along the sluice box, one on either side, alert senses probing the night, stopping every little way to listen and look. Water had been cut off from the sluice at the end of the day's shift. Now there was only a measured dripping from soaked seams. The box was a gigantic snake, running away into the dark.

"All quiet now," said Burge. "But I'm sure I heard somebody moving."

Now Teague's alerted senses were razor-sharp, and a queer, instinctive bristling was tautening up his nerve ends. It was something given to him by past training. His glance swept the dark again and again. Burge was right. Something was afoot, something was out there in the night. It wasn't that Teague heard or saw a thing. It was something that came up from within him and told him this.

"I'll stay here," he told Burge softly. "You get back and tell the others to be on their toes. Make it fast!"

Burge started to slip away. And it was at this moment that up out of the black shadow beside the sluice box a figure leaped and drove smashing into Jim Teague. A swinging blow with some kind of club barely missed Teague's head, but thudded down on his right shoulder, partially numbing it and his arm. A single hoarse call reached through the night and then men seemed to explode from all sides in the dark and closed in with a rush.

Had Jim Teague wanted to draw his gun, he could not have managed it, for that numbing blow on the shoulder had for the moment made his right hand clumsy and aimless. But of one thing he was very certain. He was literally faced with a fight for his life. That swinging club, had it landed on his head as intended, would have most certainly crushed his skull like an eggshell.

Teague did what he could with his left arm. He lashed out with it, felt his clenched fist bite against flesh and saw the club-wielding figure fall away from him. But instantly there were others all over him, clawing, smashing, cursing. By sheer force of numbers they carried him back and down, and then there were heavy boots kicking and stamping at him.

Only the dark and the fact that the attackers got in the way of one another saved Jim Teague from being kicked and stamped to a pulp, then and there. Partially gathering himself, he lunged desperately into the tangle of boots and so brought down a tripped-up pile of cursing, scrambling men. When these untangled and struggled to their feet again, Teague stumbled erect, too. Now, in the dark, the attackers were momentarily uncertain as to just who was who, and so Teague gained a little respite.

But only for a moment. Then they were after him again, like a pack of ravening wolves. Jim Teague was a fighting man. In one way or another, fighting had been pretty much his main stock in trade for a number of years. Fear he did not know, but there was a definite limit to what one man could do against many. If he could have made his right hand work and got at his gun, things might have been different. As it was, though they did not get him down again, their numbers kept on driving him back and back.

Once more it was their own press of numbers that saved him from serious injury. For anyone trying to swing a club in this wild tangle would have run as big a chance of braining one of his own group as he would of hitting Teague.

So he took mauling blows of heavy fists and got home a few himself. A man cursed in thick, blubbering rage after Teague's sound left arm had winged hard, cutting knuckles into the fellow's mouth. And, using the same weapons that the others brought, Teague drove a boot to a man's kneecap and brought him down, yelling in his agony.

A hard, booming voice shouted an order from some other spot along the sluice. Now, right after it came a pounding and crashing, the sounds of boards being splintered and riven. And Teague knew then that the raiders were tearing Rupe Caldwell's sluice boxes to pieces.

Well, there was nothing he could do about it. For he was still fighting for his life, fighting in a stark, wolfish silence, trying to husband his breath and his strength on the chance that somewhere along this rocky trail he would gain a chance to break free of this tenacious group of savage figures that kept coming steadily at him. Only sheer, cold tenacity and courage kept him on his feet. But always he had to give ground.

And then, under his spread and reeling feet the gravel bar dropped in a sudden, sharp pitch behind him. The change in level threw him off balance completely, just as a heavy, winging fist crashed into his face. He fell backward and the icy flood of the creek caught him and whirled him away!

V

CAMP PARIAH

In the smashing hurly-burly of that surprise attack, Jim Teague had not once thought of the creek, had not realized it was so close behind him. With the curses and panting imprecations of his attackers and with his head ringing from the blows he had taken, he had not heard the tossing splash of water. But now he was into it, the icy shock of it numbing and half-strangling him. For a moment all was chaos and instinctive effort on his part to get his head above the racing surface.

Then, as his head broke into the clear and he was able to fill his lungs with precious air once more, cogent thought began to function again. And instantly he realized that here might be a chance for escape which he otherwise would not have known. He was not fool enough to try and get back into the brawl. That would have done no whit of good. For this was a fight that had been lost almost as it began. So Jim Teague caught a deep, gasping breath and held it, letting the rushing waters have their own way with him, carrying him on into the night.

For some distance the attackers ran along the edge of the creek. One of them plunged in, almost to his waist, made a grab at Teague's drifting figure, but a surge and swirl of the current carried him out of reach. After that came a shower of clubs and rocks, thrown viciously but blindly. But none of them found their target and all the time the sweep of the waters gained more time and distance for Jim Teague.

The main drive of the current now made an angling sweep toward the far bank, carrying him that way. He moved and worked only enough to keep his face above water, catching a deep, aching breath now and then. Several times the power of the current slammed him against partly submerged boulders, spun him around and carried him on once more.

The sound and movement of pursuit along the creek bank faded. A voice called triumphantly, "That one's done for. He was about finished when he went in. That snow water will finish the job!"

Jim Teague realized that this might well be true, for the icy chill was biting deeper and deeper until it seemed that his very heart must freeze. He rolled over on his stomach and began to swim with the current. His left arm was sound enough, but his right was still slow and clumsy from that savage clubbing his shoulder had taken.

With the drive of the current to aid him he traveled fast. The tumult upstream grew fainter and fainter. Teague began fighting an angling way across the current, found shallowing water at last, then clawed and lurched his way up onto the bank, where he lay, panting and shaking.

Cold as the water had been, it seemed even colder out of it, the night chill striking bitterly through the soaked and sodden clamminess of clothes. Teague's teeth began to chatter, and shudder after shudder of beaten misery swept over him. He had to get up — he had to get moving. . . .

The short but savage fight, the punishment he'd taken and the blood-congealing iciness of creek waters had taken more out of him than he realized. He had to try twice, and desperately, before he could get to his feet and stay there. Even so, he was staggering and stumbling like a drunken man as he started off. It seemed as if every staggering step needed a separate effort of will and commanding mind before it could be achieved. And he had to clench his teeth savagely to keep his chin from wobbling.

But he kept at it, one step after another, until each one became a little firmer and more sure than the last.

The first hundred yards were the hardest. Then enough strength and balance had returned to enable him to break into a shuffling run to get his sluggish blood stirring once more. A second hundred yards and the numbness of chill began to fade a little. He dragged deep of the night's cold breath and kept on, moving ever freer and with more certain stride. He knew where he had to get and what he had to have. Rupe Caldwell's cabin and a roaring fire.

He dodged miner's tents, scattered across these lower flats. He stumbled over dug gravel dumps and once came near charging blindly into an open shaft. From one tent an awakened miner cursed suspiciously and came to the tent's open flap, gun in hand. But by that time Teague was yards away and hidden by the dark.

He broke clear of the flats at last, struck the upslope to town. By now the breath of concentrated effort was rasping hoarse and raw in his straining throat, but he sucked greedily at the air and kept doggedly on. Water sucked and squished in his sodden boots and his clothes were a clinging, freezing shroud. But deep in his straining chest his heart was booming strongly and carrying him on to the sanctuary he sought.

Town was empty and the cabin, when he finally staggered up to it, was dark. Teague thought he would find Caldwell there, but when, with shaking fingers, he got some matches off the grub shelf and got a lamp lighted, he saw that he had the place to himself.

He shoved fat pine kindling into the stove, got it flaming. Then, as the first sucking roar of the draft began, he stripped to the skin and went at his bare and aching flesh with a rough towel. He knew that Caldwell kept a bottle under the head of his bunk and he took a deep drag at this. He wrapped a blanket about himself and hovered over the stove, now beginning to creak with heat.

In another fifteen minutes he was as restored and comfortable as a man could hope to be who had taken the savage, wicked punishment he had. The lamplight showed him that he was a mass of bruises where club and fists and boots had landed. His right shoulder was no longer numb, but had stiffened up until he could barely raise his arm. The bruise where the club had landed was a wicked one.

Teague hung his clothes about the stove and they began to steam. He was amazed to discover that he had not lost his gun, despite all he'd been through. Tucked well under his belt, it had stayed with him, creek experience and all. So now he unloaded the weapon and put it inside the open oven of the stove to dry out. He brewed a pot of coffee and drank one steaming cup after another.

Steps came up outside the cabin and then it was Sharpe and Tappan who stumbled in. Both were beaten and bruised and bloody, staggering with exhaustion. Teague laced a couple of cups of coffee heavily from Caldwell's bottle and the two men gulped the drinks thankfully.

"Burge?" asked Teague. "What about him?"

Sharpe shrugged. "Dunno," he mumbled. "Never heard or saw nothin' of him. Didn't have time to inquire around, by God! Seemed like there was a hundred lit all over Tom and me. Never had a chance to throw a gun or do ourselves any good at all, and it wouldn't have counted a whoop if we'd tried. There was just too damn many of them, all set to beat our brains out. Dunno yet how we got clear with whole skins. Wonder what Caldwell will say?"

"Who gives a damn what he says?" blurted Tappan. "We did the best we could, and who could have done more, considerin' what hit us? I could stand another cup of that stuff, Teague."

After Sharpe and Tappan had rested and recovered somewhat, Teague said, "You fellows might as well go and turn in. There's nothing we can do about things until daylight. Wouldn't do a lick of good to go back to the diggings now, even if we had an army behind us. The damage is done. Let me worry about Rupe Caldwell. I'll take the blame for everything. I was in charge."

Alone, Teague hunched close to the stove, baking his clubbed shoulder in the heat, working and kneading the pounded muscles with his left hand, flexing and swinging the arm until gradually the worst of the stiffness was gone. From time to time he moved and turned his clothes and kept the stove stoked and roaring. Then, under the lamplight he cleaned and oiled his gun and from the box, filled the gaping chambers with fresh ammunition.

Daylight was thrusting gray fingers through the cabin window by the time Teague's clothes were dry enough to don again. He dressed, got together a bite of breakfast and was just finishing eating when Rupe Caldwell came stamping in. The smell of whiskey was strong on Caldwell, his eyes were bloodshot from sleeplessness and there was an unaccustomed surliness about him.

"Heavy poker game in the back room of the Big Nugget," he explained harshly. "And my luck was stinking. Sa-ay! Didn't you come off shift kind of early? It's barely daylight."

"Came off shift just an hour or so after midnight," said Teague quietly. "Got thrown off."

"What! You got thrown off? What do you mean?"

"Just that. A whole mob of them hit us without the slightest warning. There must have been ten to one against us and we never had a chance. Tappan and Sharpe and me managed to get out alive. Burge — I don't know. He was talking to me just a second before the attack hit. I never heard or saw anything more of him after that. I was just going down to try and find out about him. By the sound of things, they took axes to your sluice boxes, Rupe."

It took Rupe Caldwell a long moment or two to get the full implication of this. Then his lips writhed thin and a blaze of black anger suffused his bloodshot eyes. His voice went thick.

"Is that what I hired you for, to let my

sluices be raided? Damn it, Teague — I thought you were a fighting man. There were several thousand of dollars' worth of gold against the riffles of those sluice boxes. I intended to clean up this afternoon. I suppose they robbed my sluices before smashing them up?"

"I wouldn't know about that," said Teague grimly. "About that time I was too busy keeping my head from being clubbed in to get what clse was going on. I'm sorry about the whole thing, but I tell you, we never had a chance."

As realization struck deeper and deeper, Caldwell's anger grew. "Chance — hell!" he snarled. "As a fightin' man you should have made your own chances. What do you carry that gun for, pleasure? The whole thing is, I don't think you really wanted to protect my interests. I can see now that I made a mistake in ever hiring you. You just haven't got the salt necessary for this job. And you're full of a lot of weak-spined sympathy for every blundering fool miner and any snooty piece of dress goods who comes along to give you a calf-eyed glance and a simpering smile. You —"

Teague swung around, cold storminess in his eyes. "I'd go a little easy with that kind of talk if I were you, Rupe. Right now you're sore because you took a whipping at poker and there's the dregs of too much whiskey dying in you. Yeah, you got a right to be smoked-up over the raid on your sluices. But just the same, watch your tongue. Better get some sleep and cool off before you say something I won't let you get away with."

"I'll have my say right here and now," Caldwell rasped. "When I trust a man and pay him fat wages I expect results, not mealy-mouthed talk and excuses. But you never did get the right slant on this deal through your thick head, did you? Why, you've even tried to tell me what I could and what I could not do. I let you get by with that for a time, figuring you'd finally get the real picture through your skull. You pushed some of my good boys around, like George Ides and Curly Bolan. I even stood for that. But no more. You're done, Teague — through! Get out of this camp and keep going. You'll do that or —"

"Or what?" cut in Teague.

"Or you'll stay here for good."

Teague laughed and there was no mirth in it. "Rupe, you're beginning to bluster. Come down to earth. You ain't big enough to run me out of this camp, or any other."

"I brought you in here, I can run you out,"

spat Caldwell. "Yeah, I brought you in here and what were you when you arrived? Why just a down-and-out bum, without even eatin' money in your jeans. Just a damn beggar. So I gave you a break, staked you to clothes and a bunk and food to put in your belly. And you never were really with me, not from the first. So now, you get out, you soft-headed blunderer!"

The hard, cynical smile lay on Jim Teague's lips. "A man," he said cuttingly, "should always trust his instincts. I should have trusted mine, for this camp is right about you, Rupe. You're all the average miner says you are, and more. You're a damned, low-down crook, Rupe. That's what my instinct told me before I'd been in Bonanza Gulch twenty-four hours. But I tried to argue that instinct down, to give you a break and reserve judgment. So this is where the trail forks, eh? Well, I'm glad. I feel cleaner, somehow. I won't have to look slant-eyed at myself any more. Yeah, you staked me when I first hit here, but I don't feel that I owe you a cent. Because you never did give me that full picture. You covered up, lied to me. You made big smooth talk to justify all the dirty work you and your crowd have been pulling. And now you think you're going to run me out of town! Rupe, that will take some doing."

Caldwell cursed thickly. "Get out of this cabin! Go sleep in the mud where you belong and where you'd have been if I hadn't taken you in. And leave this town if you want to go on living!"

"Tough talk, Rupe," drawled Teague mockingly. "Care to try and back it up — now?"

For a moment Teague thought Caldwell would try, for his face was convulsed with a sudden hate and he rocked up on his toes like something ready to spring. But somewhere along the trail Rupe Caldwell had lost the directness of a real fighting man. He had dipped deep into scheming, devious ways to gain his ruthless ends and the habit had him by the throat. Caldwell would have to scheme this thing out, hit from an unexpected angle while holding himself safely in the background. Also, the old fiber wasn't there any more. For when a man grows soft through moral rot, then physical rot sets in, too. And his nerve goes sour. Bluntly, faced with Teague's taunting challenge, Rupe Caldwell found he didn't have the courage to go through.

Jim Teague saw all this and gave that same mirthless laugh again. "You've slipped, Rupe," he taunted. "You don't walk any more. You creep. Where's the big man now, Rupe? You know — the man who would be big like Garr Paden liked it, who claimed he had his foot on the little fellow's throat, and wanted it that way? Yeah, Rupe — you move on all fours, now. You creep, you slickery side-winder!"

"Get out!" choked Caldwell hoarsely. "Get out!"

Teague moved to the door. "Your luck's gone, Rupe. You better travel while the going is good. Because you've made an issue of this between you and me. Well, the clean, outside air will smell good. Good!"

Jim Teague opened the door and backed through it.

Bonanza Gulch boiled with the news of the night raid on Rupe Caldwell's sluice boxes. Idling about town, Jim Teague heard the talk. Miners met, discussed it, grinned and gloated openly. Most of the talk pointed to the fact that Barney Foxx had led the raid. Teague recalled the man as the powerful, black-bearded, fiery, blue-eyed miner who had ordered him off one claim at gun's point.

But down on the flats saws were whining and hammers rattling again, for Caldwell already had a crew at work, repairing what they could, rebuilding what they must. And stacked with the workers' tools were rifles, loaded and ready.

Teague spent considerable time about the trading post, where he bought a new hat, having lost his old one in the icy creek the night before. In time he ended up squatting on his heels against the side of the post, letting the morning sun bake the stiffness out of his clubbed shoulder. His thoughts ran bleak. There was little ahead of him, here in Bonanza Gulch. He had broken with Rupe Caldwell, but his former associations there had damned him in the eyes of the miners and more solid citizens of the camp. He knew the biting loneliness of the outcast.

From where he sat he could look down across the camp to the Sherrill cabin. Twice he glimpsed Janet Sherrill, once when she came out to throw away a pan of dishwater, again when she emerged to sweep the cabin step. Simple acts of everyday, commonplace housekeeping duties, yet of special significance to a lonely man.

Jack Case showed up and squatted beside him, building a cigarette. Teague said, "You're in poor company, Jack."

Case shrugged and spat. "I've been in poor company, you mean, and I don't like it. Caldwell sent out the word that you were through. He's put Bully Girard in your place. You're staying in Bonanza Gulch, Jim?"

Teague nodded. "I'm staying — for a while at least. Long enough to prove to Rupe Caldwell that he isn't big enough to run me out."

"Watch your back," said Case.

Teague swung his head, looked at Case, but Case was staring straight ahead. "You've heard talk?" asked Teague.

"No. But I can read the signs. While you were one of us, Caldwell had to keep Ides and Bolan off your neck. But now — well, you can guess what those two lovely birds would like to do. And Bully Girard is of the same breed. Or would I put it past Caldwell to sic 'em on you?"

"I'd already figured that out," said Teague drily. "But thanks, just the same."

"Something else I wanted to tell you," Case said. "Maybe it don't mean a thing. But it struck me as being kinda queer. Last night when I came off shift I stopped in at the Big Nugget for a little time before turning in. When I did head up for the cabin, two fellows on horses nearly rode me down in the dark. They were headin' out of town. I was down close to the ground where it was dark and they couldn't recognize me. But I got a fair look at them against the stars.

127

George Ides and Curly Bolan. Now what would those two have been doing, heading out of town and on horseback?"

Teague stiffened slightly. "Sure of them, were you, Jack?"

Case nodded. "Positive. So I'm wondering."

"So," murmured Teague, "am I."

Again his thoughts reached back to a looted stage standing on a mountain road, with a driver and a shotgun guard lying dead, with a treasure box shot open, with the sign of two horses near by, and of an empty revolver shell, calibre .44 Russian.

Case got to his feet. "If you hear anything, Jim, that I don't, let me know. I'm willing to risk my skin in an open, up-and-down fight for a couple of gold claims, but I've no wish to be tied up with any outfit that is downright murderous crooked. That could lead to a rope around my neck and, while mine may not amount to much in the eyes of some, still and all I'm kinda partial to it because it's the only one I have." Case grinned twistedly.

Teague said, "I'll let you know, Jack. I surely will."

Case thought of something else. "You hear about Burge?" he asked.

Teague shook his head. "No. But I've

been wondering. What about him?"

"That raid last night really put the fear of God in him, I reckon," said Case. "He came sneaking up to the cabin just at daylight, got his gear together and caught a ride out with a freighter heading across the mountains to Timber Lodge. I asked him what the idea was. He said that when the miners began acting in organized bunches, it was a good time to get scarce."

"Maybe he was wise, at that," said Teague.

Case spat, rubbed his lips with the back of his hand. "I'm going to watch all signs mighty close."

Case went on his way and Jim Teague dropped back into the shadow of his thoughts. Sheriff Wade Riker came down the street from the Big Nugget, dark, stony-faced, black-eyed. He gave Teague a slanting glance and turned into the trading post. A moment later Janet Sherrill came out of her father's cabin and moved in toward town, quick stepping, lithe, pretty in the sunshine. She also was headed toward the Post.

Jim Teague got to his feet, touched his hat. His voice reached across to her, low and quiet. "I still say, don't let Riker get hold of that injunction. If he does, it will end up in

Rupe Caldwell's hands and you'll never see it again. Have a committee of miners serve it for you."

She flashed him a glance, seeing a tall man with grave, still features. She colored faintly, made as if to speak, but instead faced straight ahead and hurried on into the trading post. A couple of minutes later she came out again and with her was Wade Riker. They went down across town to the Sherrill cabin.

Jim Teague's brooding glance followed them. He tried to tell himself that it didn't matter, that he didn't care. What was this girl to him, anyhow? Why should he concern himself or interest himself in any way over her affairs? She was just someone he had met by chance, an acquaintanceship as sketchy as it was brief. For that matter, what right had he to interfere? Who was he to think that it would matter?

He had hit this boom town, just as down and out as Rupe Caldwell had said. He was little better off now, if any. Then at least he was in position to have a respectable job offered him, in fact, a job of trust and responsibility, like driving a stage carrying a treasure box. But now he was an outcast, a pariah. He was done with Rupe Caldwell's organization, but he was also a marked man with the honest element of the camp and they wanted no part of him.

He had, he realized now, been a fool to be taken in by Rupe Caldwell's glib, too hearty talk, and with his promises of big money. He should have realized when Caldwell tossed that fifty ounce poke in front of him that here was nothing honest and that when he accepted the gold he was tying himself up with something that was shady and crooked. Then there was the kind of men Caldwell had surrounded himself with. A crew of cutthroats like George Ides and Curly Bolan and Bully Girard. These alone, Teague mused bitterly, should have been enough to warn him off.

Well, he had gone over these things in his mind before and now, as he mentally stacked them up for another look and, with the clearer picture of Rupe Caldwell as he really was, which the past few hours had furnished, Teague marveled that he could have been taken in the way he had been. His self-disgust grew.

Of course, in extenuation, there was the fact that a man's physical and mental condition could greatly affect his judgment at any given moment. When he was down and out, broke, weak and cold and hungry, a man was apt to be more concerned with such fundamentals as food and shelter and warm clothes than he was with a fine distinction between what was right and what was wrong. Particularly could this be so when he did not know all the truth or, in fact, any great part of it concerning a situation.

Again a great revulsion against this gold camp of Bonanza Gulch swept over Jim Teague. Riches might be here for some, ill-gained or otherwise, but not for him. This wasn't his element and he was out of place here. He belonged on the open running plains, a good horse under him, and cattle out in front or all around him. That was his life. And if there be conflict, even life and death battles, there was still a kind of rugged, fundamental honesty about such fighting. The issues were clear-cut and a man chose his side and that was that. He knew where he stood and he knew where the other fellow stood.

Here there was trickery and here there were lies. Here men were knifed in their blankets and their pokes stolen. Here was the unbalance of perspective and principle which the sight of raw gold produced. Even among the so-called better element of the miners there was no sure way of telling how much of their stand was based on principle and how much on greed for that mocking, yellow metal.

Teague got to his feet and shook himself. There was no profit in trying to analyze things that had been or things that might have been. Water flowed under a bridge but once. The past was history and there were problems of the present to be faced.

Here he was in Bonanza Gulch and, hating the place or not, here he was going to stay until Rupe Caldwell got fully over the idea he could drive him out. But while he stayed he had to eat and he had to find a place to sleep. And while he still had some of those fifty ounces left — they wouldn't last forever. He had to find a job of some sort.

A lift of recklessness swept through him and he crossed over to the stage station. He found Ben App talking to a miner with rippling black-beard and fierce blue eyes. Barney Foxx. They broke off in their talk and stared at him coldly. Barney Foxx had a dark and swollen bruise under one eye and Teague knew that this was a memento of the sluice box raid.

Ben App spoke curtly. "Have your say and make it brief. I got little time to waste on such as you."

"Maybe," said Teague quietly. "The first day I hit here you offered me the job as stage driver. I imagine by this time you've found a man for that. But if you could use another

133

man around at something connected with horses, you might consider me. I savvy horses and can handle them."

Ben App stared at him as though he had not heard rightly. "You!" he burst out. "You're asking me for a job? Of all the crazy, damned nonsense —"

"Is it?" cut in Teague. "What makes it so?"

"Why," exploded Ben App, "do you think I'd have a Caldwell man working for me? Of all the cussed, brassbound nerve! Mister, if I needed a thousand men, not one of them would be a man who had ever taken Caldwell's pay."

"But I'm not a Caldwell man," explained Teague. "I was, but no longer. Caldwell and me don't see alike. I had to work for him a while to find that out."

Barney Foxx grinned mockingly. "Found last night a little too rugged for you, maybe?"

"No. I've taken whippings before, will probably take them again. I was just wondering if I put that eye on you? I landed a few good ones."

Barney Foxx spat derisively. "I've been telling the boys that Caldwell's crowd wasn't near as tough as they let on to be. Just a bunch of coyotes, trailing after another coyote who thinks he's a wolf. What an awakening he's got coming!"

A wintry bleakness began forming in Jim Teague's eyes, but he held on to the surge of temper that began to burn in him. "I wouldn't know about that." He looked at Ben App again. "I'd sure like to have that job, friend. You have my word for it that you won't be sorry."

Ben App held Teague's glance for a long moment, then shook his head, his tone and manner going slightly milder. "You had your chance. But you signed on with the wrong bunch."

Teague shrugged and turned away. At that moment a man stuck his head in the door and called excitedly.

"Come a-runnin', Ben. Here's Bob Porter, just rode into town and he's all shot to rags!"

Ben App exclaimed. "Bob Porter? The gold messenger, Barney! Good Lord — do you suppose — ?"

Ben App hurried out, with Barney Foxx crowding his heels. Jim Teague followed them, slowly.

A horse had just come to a stop before the stage station. In its saddle a man was humped over the saddle horn, swaying from side to side, clinging to the horn with both hands. Those hands were dark with dried blood. The front of his shirt was drenched with the same dread dark stain. At the base of the man's neck and to one side, bright crimson welled from an open wound.

"Bob!" cried Ben App. "What happened, man? Here, Barney — give me a hand with him!"

They would have lifted him down, but the man in the saddle shook his head in slow, vague swings. His voice was just a croak, coming as though from some great distance.

"No! Listen — for time's runnin' — out. Two of them jumped me — just after daylight. They were masked — hid out along the trail. I — never had a chance for they started — right in shootin'. Don't know how — I got away. At the first shot — the light seemed to go out. Next I knew I — was still in the saddle, my horse — runnin'. I just hung on —"

The speaker swayed widely, weaving.

Barney Foxx and Ben App, reaching up, steadied him. "The pack horses, Bob?" urged Barney Foxx. "What about the pack horses with the treasure?"

That far-off croak moved still further away, until it was just a breathing echo.

"Don't know — don't know — !"

Of a sudden all substance seemed to melt out of the man. He was a limp and sliding bundle when Barney Foxx and Ben App caught him. His head lolled, his arms hung loosely. He was dead.

Jim Teague watched Barney Fox and Ben App carry the treasure messenger into the stage station, then moved away, heading for the group of Caldwell cabins. He found Moulton and Hamper in one of them. He asked for Jack Case and was told that Case was probably at the Big Nugget, so he went there.

He found Case sitting at an idle poker table, killing time at a game of solitaire. Teague dropped into a chair across from him. "Keep right on playing, Jack," Teague murmured. "But listen close. I promised to tell you things. What do you think of this?"

Teague told of what he'd just seen and heard at the stage station. Case's movements, as he had laid down card after card, became slower and more deliberate.

"Two of them, eh?" he said softly. "Two of them jumped that messenger and got away with the treasure. And there were two of them I saw riding out of town last night around midnight. George Ides and Curly Bolan — riding where?"

"And there was two of them who held up that stage the day I first came in to this camp," nodded Teague. "Jack, the pattern grows pretty plain."

"Too plain for me," said Case. "I know

when I've had a big plenty. You're already through with Rupe Caldwell. Now I am. Much obliged for looking me up and telling me this, Jim. Burge was smart. Wish I'd ridden that same freight wagon out of town. Where do we go from here?"

A door slammed open. A man at the bar, laughing at some remark the bartender had made, went suddenly silent, his laugh breaking off into a thin, whistling gasp of alarm. Jim Teague's head snapped up.

In the open door of that side room that was Rupe Caldwell's headquarters, stood a hulking, red-headed, redbearded animal of a man. Bully Girard, his eyes burning crimson with the lust of killing. Just settling against his shoulder was a sawed-off shotgun, the twin muzzles swinging in line with Jim Teague's chest.

Teague's reactions were instinctive, explosive, product of the rough, dangerous years of the past. His hands were on the edge of the table, as he had leaned forward in his brief talk with Jack Case. So now, in one tremendous surge, Teague threw the table up and over, knocking Case backward out of his chair. With the same move, Teague fell sideways out of his own chair.

The shotgun that Bully Girard held, roared wickedly.

VI

HIGH TREASURE

At a time of high stress and danger, the minds of men are unpredictable. With some the mind ties up, growing numb and stupefied, leaving them hopeless and helpless. But with others their thoughts flash with split-second, razor-keen perception. And with still others sheer speed of thought combines with blazing instinct. So it was with Jim Teague.

His move in upsetting the table to make the most of its flimsy protection had been sheer instinct, done without conscious thought or calculation. But as he fell from his chair, driving himself sideways, his thoughts were alive, lightning flashes ripping across his brain.

Here, he knew, was the tightest spot he'd ever been in in all his life, a life that had seen plenty of tight clutches. If he managed to evade that first treacherous charge of buckshot, he would be only half done. For there was a second barrel to that shotgun which Bully Girard held and Girard had only to swing the weapon a trifle, twitch the trigger and send a second charge of buckshot ripping its deadly way. Yet there was the recoil of the shotgun on that first shot, recoil which would hammer against Girard's shoulder and toss the muzzle of the weapon up. That would slow Girard a trifle in getting away the second shot — just a trifle. But in a split-second affair like this a man's life could hang on a trifle. . . .

Teague had drawn his gun as he fell, another move that was pure instinctive reaction. Now the force of his sideways lunge sent him sliding along the floor on his left side, so that his head and shoulders and extended right arm and gun, shoved clear, past the bulk of the table.

Bully Girard had been animal-sure of his target — too sure. He had seen the breadth of Jim Teague's chest over the muzzle of his shotgun and it was something he felt he couldn't miss. Yet, even as he had begun pressing the trigger, the poker table upset and his target fell away from in front of him, too fast for him to correct his aim. And it was at that moment that the trigger gave under the pressure of his finger and the shotgun roared.

At this short range the charge of buckshot had little chance to spread and its compactness would have torn a man almost in half, had it hit. But it did not hit Jim Teague. It hit where he had been, that split second before. The upthrown edge of the poker table took the full impact.

A gout of splintered wood and shreds of green felt flew upward. Girard, knowing he had missed where he'd felt he could not, cursed thickly and fought the shotgun's recoil, pulling the uptossed muzzle down and back into line, intended to rake the area close to the floor with his second shot.

The heavy Colt gun in Jim Teague's extended right hand roared its own challenge. It was a snap shot, pure and simple, calculated to upset and confuse more than with any real hope of hitting fatally. Yet, the slug did it. It smashed into Bully Girard's left arm, just below the bent elbow, the blow tearing Girard's supporting hand from the fore-end of the shotgun, allowing the muzzle of the weapon to drop, and the sagging weight of the gun came fully upon the finger which Girard had curled around the second trigger.

The gun smashed out its second discharge and the load of buckshot gouged into the floor not two yards from Bully Girard's spread feet. Girard dropped the gun, catching at his wounded arm. He tried to dodge back through the door of the side room.

But Jim Teague was up on his left elbow now, and lining up a second shot with certainty. He had Girard clearly over his sights and he drove a slug into the very center of Bully Girard's hulking body. Girard swayed and fell against the doorpost, clawing at it with his sound hand, trying to hold himself erect. A third bullet hammered into Girard's chest, heart-high. Girard tipped away from the support, fell heavily on his face.

Jim Teague was on his feet, dragging Jack Case from under the wreckage of the table. "You all right, Jack?"

"All right," mumbled Case. "Girard — what set him off?"

Teague did not answer. He was already headed across to the open door of that side room. He leaped over and past Bully Girard's sprawled figure without a glance. Now indeed was the icy storm seething and swirling in Teague's eyes. He was set for anything as he went through that door.

The room was empty. Teague whirled back, plugging fresh loads into his gun. At a white-faced, staring bartender, he threw a single harsh, questioning word. "Caldwell?"

The bartender shrugged, running the tip of his tongue over dry lips. "Not here. Left a good hour ago."

"Where?"

"I dunno. He didn't say."

Jim Teague swept the room with a savage glance. The door of the Big Nugget swung back and Sheriff Wade Riker came hurrying in. He stabbed a black-eyed glance at the upturned poker table, at Bully Girard's sprawled stillness and then his eyes raked Jim Teague.

"What's going on here?" he rapped harshly. He jerked his head toward Girard. "You responsible for that?"

"Why not?" retorted Teague coldly. "He asked for it. He opened the show."

"So you say. By the look of Bully, he can't tell his side."

"Take it or leave it." Teague laid the words down flatly. "Next play is yours."

Wade Riker's black eyes flickered and settled on the bartender. "How did you see it, Frank?"

"The truth," warned Jim Teague, "and nothing but the truth, so help you!"

The bartender shrugged. "Bully came out a-shootin', Wade. And he just wasn't good enough."

"Satisfied?" Teague asked of Riker.

Riker did not answer, but went over to Girard. Teague jerked his head to Jack Case and went out of the Big Nugget, Case following. When they reached the street, Case spoke in an awed tone.

"Man! Now I know why Rupe Caldwell wanted you on his side. He made a mistake in not keeping you."

"He couldn't have kept me," Teague said thinly. "Because he's a smooth-talking, crooked, double-dealing rat. And I want him!"

"You figure he set Bully Girard after you?"

"Of course he did. There never was any love lost between Girard and me from the first day we met. Yet I've had little to do with him. He had no reason of his own to set out to get me. When Caldwell and I had our little understanding, Caldwell told me to get out of town, or stay here for good. This was what he meant. Well, we'll see who stays in Bonanza Gulch for good."

Jack Case studied Teague with a slanted glance, marked the frigid tumult in Teague's eyes and the rigid tautness of his face.

"I don't blame you for feeling as you do, Jim. But don't you forget that Rupe Caldwell's got quite an organization built up. Maybe the smart thing for you to do would be to get enough backing to smash that organization first before going after Caldwell."

Teague barked a short, mirthless laugh.

"Who would I find in this camp to back me? You forget that I was a Caldwell man, once. So there isn't a decent man in Bonanza Gulch who'd trust me as far as he could spit. And I can't blame him."

Case shrugged. "That could be true. But you can't be sure of it until you try. Caldwell won't be long in hearing that Bully Girard messed up his little chore. He'll know that you'll have all the angles figured and he'll be doubly on his guard, with men laying for you from all sides. One of them gets you, then Caldwell will be more firmly in the saddle than ever. I'd say now was a good time to outsmart him, outthink him."

The first blaze of stark anger was fading a little in Jim Teague, letting the wisdom of Jack Case's words sink in. He nodded slowly.

"I'll give it one more try. But if it don't work, why then I go after Caldwell alone and I'll either get him or he'll get me. Now, what about you? You're pulling out on Caldwell, yourself. We've been seen together, you and me. That will put Caldwell after you, too."

"I'm small fry," said Case. "I don't rate much. I had thought of pulling out of this camp, but the way things are beginning to shape up I think I'll stick around a little longer. I might come in handy somewhere. I'll do a lot of looking and listening. Now you get busy. And watch yourself, Jim."

Jim Teague went straight back to the stage station again and was in luck to find Ben App alone. The stage agent began to bristle, but Teague said swiftly, "You and me are going to have a talk, App. I got a proposition and you're going to listen to it."

"Not interested," snapped Ben App. "I thought I'd made it plain that I want no truck with you, Teague."

"Just the same," stated Teague flatly, "you're going to listen. Please get it through your head that I'm not a Caldwell man any more. If you want proof of that, find out what happened in the Big Nugget just now."

The stout little stage agent stared at Teague with puckered eyes. "I thought I heard some shooting up that way," he admitted. "What happened?"

"Bully Girard tried to get me with a sawed-off shotgun. A sneak play. And it didn't work."

"Where's Girard now?"

"Dead. I'm positive Caldwell set him after me, for it's exactly in line with the threat Caldwell made when he and I split up."

"What threat?"

Teague told him and Ben App said, a

slight sneer in his voice, "What brought on the row between Caldwell and you? Wasn't he splitting the stake fairly enough to suit you?"

Teague rolled his head from side to side. "Give me patience, Lord!" he gritted. "I thought this man App was smart. I thought he had enough common sense to recognize the truth if he saw it and was big enough to listen when a man is laying that truth on the line!"

Ben App gave Teague another long, searching stare. Then he nodded. "All right, I'm listening. Have your say."

Jim Teague gave him the story, briefly and tersely, right from the first, telling of where he'd first met Rupe Caldwell, of the letter Caldwell had written him and the proposition Caldwell put up to him when he first hit Bonanza Gulch.

"I'm making no excuses, understand," Teague explained. "But I was down and out. I needed something to eat, a bunk to sleep in, some decent clothes on my back. And a man in that condition doesn't always show the best of judgment. The proposition Caldwell offered me didn't seem too much out of line at that time. It shaped up pretty much as an up-and-down fight between men over the ownership of some placer

147

claims, the true titles of which were in doubt. I'd done my share of fighting for chunks of cattle range where the actual legitimate ownership was in doubt and this listened something the same. So I took Caldwell's pay and sided with him."

Ben App nodded slowly. "I can understand how that would be. Go on."

"Well," resumed Teague, "things happened. I heard things and I saw things that didn't shape up right according to my judgment. I began to realize that Caldwell had pulled me into something with his smooth talk and big pay. I began to get my neck up. I slapped a couple of his pet thugs around, George Ides and Curly Bolan. Caldwell didn't like this, but he didn't say too much about it just then. I told Caldwell there were things he was figuring to do that I wouldn't stand for. He knew I was getting wise to him. But the open break didn't come until he tore into me because I didn't stop that raid on his sluice boxes. At that, I'd have stopped it if I could, but the odds were such that I never had a chance. So the blow-up came and, well — there's the story."

"Interesting," admitted Ben App drily. "But just what do you expect me to do about it?"

"Listen a little more." And then Teague

went on to tell of his conviction that at least one of the men who had pulled the stage holdup on the Bonanza Gulch-Timber Lodge road, had been George Ides, and he told why. Finally he told of George Ides and Curly Bolan being seen riding out of town the previous night.

At this a gleam of real interest came into Ben App's eyes. "That poor devil, Bob Porter — he said there were two of them who jumped him. And the two could have been Ides and Bolan. That's what you're driving at?"

"Right!" nodded Teague. "That's how it looks to me. What else would have sent those two riding in the night — George Ides in particular? For he's a gambler, not a night rider, unless for some pretty important reason. Oh, I'm guessing, sure. In a thing like this a man always has to do a considerable amount of guessing. But, you add up and you subtract and you come to some kind of an answer. So that's my answer until a better one comes along."

Ben App took a short turn up and down the room. "It's logical reasoning," he admitted. "But we need proof."

"Exactly! And that's the proposition I came to offer you. That you give me the chance to get that proof."

"How do you propose to go about it?"

Teague shrugged. "Simple enough. The day I hit this camp I heard you tell Wade Riker that horses left tracks. That was when you told him to get out and do something about that stage robbery. Well, you never spoke truer words. Horses do leave tracks. In my time I've seen a lot of them and on more than one occasion have followed them on pretty grim business. In other words, I've read a lot of trail sign and can do it again. I'd like the chance to look over the scene of that gold messenger holdup and see what I can find. To do that, I'll need a horse and riding gear."

Ben App scrubbed his chin furiously. "And once you had that horse and saddle, what's to keep you from riding and keeping right on riding so that I'd never see you or the horse and outfit again?"

"You believe me or you don't," stated Teague quietly. "I've put all my cards on the table. Try to understand that I've bought into this deal against Rupe Caldwell. Every man has some pride. Mine won't let me run from Caldwell's threats. Again, Caldwell set Bully Girard on me. Well, I don't take that sort of thing from any man. And maybe I got pride enough to want to square myself in the eyes of the better people of this camp."

Again their glances locked and the cold hostility that had been in Ben App's eyes was gone, now.

"I saw you cut George Ides down to size that day he and Forsythe were annoying Janet Sherrill out in the street yonder," said the stage agent. "I liked you for that, Teague. I told myself that a man had come to Bonanza Gulch. Later, I had cause to doubt that judgment. But now it looks that I could have been right after all. I'm going to gamble that I was. I'm going to trust you, Teague — believe you. I've got to believe somebody around here who has a plan and is willing to see it through. Because I've got to find some way to move treasure out of this camp safely, or go out of business. And Sheriff Wade Riker doesn't seem to be doing any good at making travel safer."

"Riker," said Teague bluntly, "is a Caldwell man. Surely you must have guessed that by this time?"

"I've had my suspicions about him," conceded Ben App. "But I'm by nature a cautious man. I don't like to jump at conclusions, though it seems I did with you. Anyhow, that's why I've told Barney Foxx to go slow in trying to stir up the miners too much. For if they got started on a lynching bee there's no telling where they'd stop, and there might be some innocent necks stretched. Which is something no decent man wants to consider. But once we get proof against some of these fellows — proof beyond any shadow of doubt, why then I'll be all for a miners' court and proper punishment. For that is the healthy way to clean up a camp. But I want that proof! And you think you can furnish it?"

"I can make an awful good try at it."

"When do you want to leave?"

"No sense in putting it off a minute, or in letting trail sign get too cold."

"Very well," said App. "I'll order up a good horse and riding outfit for you."

The stage agent went out back and Teague heard him calling orders to a hostler. When he came back, Ben App spread a piece of paper on a table and with a pencil sketched a rude map.

"During the worst of last winter," he explained, "Blizzard Pass was blocked with snow. The camp had to eat, so supplies were brought in by pack train over the old Meeker Trail. When we talked over sending out a special treasure messenger the other night, we decided to play safe and keep him off the Blizzard Pass road. We agreed to send him out over the Meeker Trail. But that didn't do us any good. They caught him anyway and you saw how it was with Bob Porter when he came in. Here's the lay of the Shawmut Mountains." Ben App, sketched lines and curves while speaking.

"Here is Blizzard Pass, over which the regular stage and freight road runs between here and Timber Lodge. The Meeker Trail runs through Vining Canyon, some six or eight miles to the west. You can't miss the trail or the canyon either if you head due west from here along the base of the Shawmuts. Somewhere along the Meeker Trail is the spot where Bob Porter was jumped. It'll be up to you, Teague, to find the exact spot and work out your sign from there. I hope it is good sign and I hope it really leads somewhere. Poor Bob Porter! I'd give ten years of my life to know how the word got out that he was making that trip. There must have been a leak somewhere. Because there would hardly have been any purpose in a couple of holdup thugs laying out along the Meeker Trail unless they knew for certain treasure was going out that way."

"Of course not," nodded Teague. "By the way, just who did know that Porter was making the trip?"

"Outside of Bob himself, just four of us. Myself, Barney Foxx, Tim McCord and

Les Jardeen. And certainly none of us would spread the word."

Jim Teague stiffened slightly, his eyes taking on a narrowing recollection. He built a cigarette with slow care, tucked it into his lips.

"Remember what I just said about adding and subtracting and finding some kind of answer? Well, see if you can add or subtract anything out of this. Last night I was in the Big Nugget, killing time before going on guard shift down at the sluices. I saw Les Jardeen come in. He went back to the dance floor for one dance. Then he left. Pretty soon I saw the girl he'd been dancing with go into Caldwell's side room. When she came out a few moments later she stopped by George Ides, who was lookout at the faro game. She spoke to Ides, who right away got another houseman to take over his place, while he went into the side room. And later last night, George Ides and Curly Bolan were seen riding out of town. Yeah, go ahead and add and subtract with that."

"Good Lord, man!" exclaimed Ben App in high agitation. "Do you realize what you're suggesting?"

"I'm not suggesting a thing," said Teague. "I'm merely telling you what I saw."

Again the stage agent started pacing the

room. Presently he stopped. "What time was this?"

"Around ten o'clock."

"We met," growled App, "at nine o'clock. It took us only about half an hour to decide on our plans. Bob Porter was to leave at three this morning, when the camp would be sure to be asleep, with little chance of anyone noting his departure. But Ides and Bolan left town around midnight, which would give them plenty of time to get set along the trail and wait for him. There was considerable dead weight in the gold the pack horses were carrying, so Bob Porter couldn't move too fast. It was daylight before he reached Vining Canyon. Yeah, all that time checks. But this other — !"

Ben App resumed his restless pacing. "After we'd once decided on our plans there was no reason for hanging on, though Barney Foxx and Tim McCord did stay, talking over other camp problems with me until eleven o'clock at least. But Les Jardeen left around nine-thirty. We never gave that a thought. Man — I tell you, I can't believe that of Les!"

Jim Teague sucked a final inhale on his cigarette, spun the butt through the open door. "The word got out, didn't it? And there is nothing so convenient as having a spy in the other fellow's camp."

"But Les Jardeen has been living with Duff Sherrill, caring for him while he was laid up. He's the last man in the world —"

"Exactly!" cut in Teague. "The last man in the world to suspect would be the best spy in the world. By your own reasoning you eliminate all who were in on the know but Les Jardeen. Ben, there's no telling what some men will do for money."

Ben App's plump shoulders sagged wearily. "I could damn you, Jim Teague," he said harshly. "I always liked Les Jardeen. Get out of here, before you have me suspecting myself."

Teague smiled grimly. "You'll keep all this between you and me? You won't tell a soul — especially not Mister Les Jardeen?"

"I won't say a word. If anybody notices you leaving and asks me about it, I'll tell them you offered to buy a horse and outfit from me and that I let you have it just to get rid of you."

Abruptly Ben App spun around and put out his hand. "Shake! And good luck!"

The afternoon was well gone when Jim Teague found the place along the Meeker Trail where the treasure messenger, Bob Porter, had run into ambush. At this place

Vining Canyon was narrow, the bottom of it hardly more than a hundred yards across, though fairly level and timber-grown. The forest mould was soft and dark underfoot. On the west side a narrow creek gorge was cut, its banks thickly crowded with low, moist-smelling shrubs and vine thickets. Shadows lay heavy, blue and shifting as smoke.

The sign was plain enough. On first striking into the mouth of the canyon, Teague could see the tracks of Porter's saddle mount and of the two pack animals — clean-cut and unhurried, heading due south — which had carried the treasure. And over this same stretch were the gouging, plunging hoofprints of Porter's saddle mount where it had come racing back, carrying the mortally wounded gold messenger.

At the exact scene of the holdup there was a wild confusion of hoof-marks, where startled horses had whirled and spun, where two had dashed off the trail and away through the timber, with the sign of two other horses racing after them, converging from above and below to head them off.

Teague reconstructed the scene in his mind as it must have been. A sudden volley of shots which had sent lead tearing through

Bob Porter. The pack animals, carrying the gold, spooking and racing away, with the two holdups spurring after them, for it was the gold that counted with the holdups. Shooting down Bob Porter had just been incidental with them. It was the treasure that they wanted. Apparently they had believed that Bob Porter, fatally wounded, could not stay long in his saddle, so, when his mount whirled and raced back along the trail, they had made no effort to follow. But they had grossly underestimated the dogged, heroic courage of Bob Porter who, though dying in the saddle, had held true to his trust.

He put this picture behind him and concentrated on what lay ahead. He found where the holdups had caught up with and cornered the pack horses. Then there was the sign to follow where, leading the pack animals, they had moved back to the Meeker Trail and turned south along it, following the run of the canyon's windings.

For a good two miles they held to the trail, then cut away from it up a gloomy side gulch that climbed and climbed toward the lofty rock rim which crested the canyon on the east. In time the gulch led out of the timber into a bleak, gray wilderness of cliff and spire and tangled slide rock. Here the sign grew faint and hard to follow directly, but

Teague was not concerned about this, for the conformation of the canyon wall right here was such that there was only one place the holdups could have topped the rim, which was a break in the barrier above a wide fan of slide rock.

It was slow, hard going, this climb, and part of the way Teague left his saddle and made it on foot, his horse scrambling up behind him. Sun's last rays were gilding this lofty rim when Teague finally topped out and he used this brief remaining light to search for and find, in a little patch of thin and rocky soil not far back from the rim, the hoof-marks of four horses, heading east.

That way ran a stretch of fairly flat tableland, scantily forested with gaunt and storm-stunted timber. Breathing his horse, Teague studied the country carefully, judging from the conformation of things the probable route of the holdups. Here things could get difficult, for there was little daylight left and a trail could easily be lost, once the forming dusk thickened. It could very well be that he would have a long, cold night to spend up in this wilderness. But if that was the way it had to be, that was the way it would be. For he wouldn't leave this trail until he had run it through to the end.

Once again in the saddle he traveled

slowly, with ever-increasing caution and alertness. All the old instincts were at work in him as he moved away toward the east. He struck a long slope which pitched down into a series of tangled ridges, low and haphazard in their aimless running this way and that. Here the timber thickened and in this the dusk became darkness.

Teague pushed slowly on, crossing several of these tangled ridges until finally, cresting one of the higher ones he came out of the timber and saw that the first stars were beginning to wink, bright and cold. He pulled up, resigned to the fact that he must wait out the night, for if he pushed ahead now he might easily overrun and lose the sign he was following. For there was no telling at what moment the trail could turn abruptly north or south.

It was plain that the holdups knew this country, had some definite destination in mind and were heading for it. Where that destination might be, Teague could only guess. It might even be Bonanza Gulch, though this was hardly probable, not with those two pack horses which Ben App could so easily identify. Well, there was only one sure way to play this thing, and that was to wait it out, pick up the trail again in tomorrow's daylight and follow it through.

A slight push of wind, moving in from the east, fanned Teague's face. It had a premonitory bite to it, that wind had, presaging a cold, cold night at this altitude. The most shelter to be found, Teague reasoned, would be back in the depths of one of the shallow gulches he'd just crossed. He started to swing his horse and ride back. Then he brought up the animal and stood high in his saddle, his face into the flow of that wind. His nostrils twitched.

Wood smoke! The smell of it, riding on that wind. Teague waited and waited, making sure. Cold exultation whipped through him. A fire burning, somewhere ahead and not too far away. And where fires burned, there humans would be. Maybe he could finish this trail tonight, after all!

He sent his horse ahead, slowly and carefully. He dipped down off this ridge, pushed through some timber, climbed another crest. From here he picked up that smell of smoke again, stronger now. Two more short flats of timber and two more ridges he topped. And now, below and ahead, there was a larger flat, where the timber broke away and let the growing reach of the starlight silver a small mountain meadow. And at the far side of the meadow, yellow light gleamed, a square of it, outlining a window.

161

And now the smell of wood smoke was strong indeed.

Jim Teague stepped out of his saddle, tied his horse in the shelter of the timber. To the saddle which Ben App had furnished him with was strapped a scabbarded rifle. Teague pulled this clear, swung the lever carefully and felt a cartridge slide into the chamber of the weapon. He lowered the hammer and then moved off through the timber to the meadow's edge, where he paused to study again the lay of things before him.

Up here the light of the stars was a silver radiance, against which the shadow under the timber was a deep, velvet black. But that swimming radiance now outlined the structure of a cabin around the square of light.

Teague was too old a hand at this sort of thing to make the mistake of heading directly across the meadow to the cabin. Instead, he circled the meadow, using the timber shadows for cover. He took his time. There was no hurry about this business, now. Whoever was in that cabin would be sitting down to eat about now. And there was no better time for a surprise move.

Teague had been circling to come in on the cabin on the side away from that window. Now, when he was within fifty yards of the place, he realized he'd chosen the wrong side, after all. For here, on this side he glimpsed the shift of movement, heard the stamp of a hoof — a small pole corral, with horses in it. And if anything alarmed those horses, that alarm could easily carry into the cabin.

So Teague retraced his steps, making the whole circle of the meadow to come back in at the cabin from the window side. He was like an Indian, now. With each step he felt carefully of what was underfoot before putting his full weight down. For as he moved ever closer to the cabin he now saw that there was no sash in that window. It was merely an opening, that could be closed by a sliding shutter of heavy, split planks. Any sound could carry through that opening, just as sounds now came out of it. The growling murmur of voices and the odors of bacon in the pan and coffee in the pot.

Like some vague shadow. Teague drifted up to a rear corner of the cabin. For a little time he waited there, every sense keening the night. Satisfied at last that there was no guard outside this place, he moved away from the cabin again, circling out and back until he could get a good look through that window without the light from within reaching far enough to touch him. This cabin stood close to the ground and so

Teague was able to get some idea of what was in it.

On the far side of the interior a rude shelflike table was built against the wall. Here a candle, stuck into the neck of a bottle, burned palely. Now, as Teague watched, a man's head and shoulders came into view, bending over the tale. The man was bearded, shaggy of head. The light of the candle threw his profile into bold relief. He had a great cruel beak of a nose and his eyes were set deep under shaggy brows.

This man swung his head and growled a summons. There was a creaking and a stir and a second man's head and shoulders moved up to the table. The first man, Jim Teague had never before laid eyes on that he could recollect. But there was no mistaking the second. Curly Bolan!

There were no others than these two and they bent over the table and began to eat.

For a long moment Jim Teague watched them, fixing their position exactly in his mind. Then he stole around to the cabin door. He laid his rifle on the ground, drew his short gun. This, when it came, would be close, fast work. A six-shooter was the weapon for that kind of business. With his left hand, Teague softly explored the door and its latch.

The latter was a sliding bar with a transverse peg reaching through a slot in the door, so that the bar could be slid back and forth from inside or out. There was no telling whether or not some kind of an additional lock held the door secure on the inside. Teague doubted that there was, but he could not be sure. If there was, then any attempt to move the sliding bar would certainly alert the pair inside and then there would be a knotty problem to handle. For that matter, things could be tough enough, even if the door opened to his first touch.

Maybe it would be smarter to move back to the window and get the drop on Bolan and his companion from there. But would a mere drop do any good? These would be tough, dangerous, reckless men. And while it would be simple enough to smoke them down through that open window without warning, that wasn't Teague's way. He could be as tough as the next one when he had to be, but he was no gulcher, no conscienceless killer.

Even as he posed the question in his mind it was settled for him. For through the door he caught a growling comment about the night's increasing chill. Then there was movement across the cabin and the rasp of wood sliding on wood and Teague knew that

165

either Bolan or the other had closed the window shutter. So now there was nothing else left but to gamble with this door.

Jim Teague had come too far along this trail to back away from it now. A cold, singing tension began whipping him, sharpening his every thought and reflex. He drew a deep breath, threw strength into a sideways drag on the bar peg. The bar slid easily, slamming back. The door gave and Teague drove it open with a crash, going through it with a long stride, his gun stabbing level. His order reached ahead of him, in hard, ringing words.

"Don't anybody move!"

For a long second they obeyed, only their heads jerking up and around. Then Curly Bolan threw himself over and back, his left hand sweeping out as he fell. He knocked the candle over, snuffed it. Except for the faint glow of a small bed of fading coals on the hearth of the rude fireplace at the far end of the cabin, all was a black and breathless dark.

VII

THE DARK ACE

Sheriff Wade Riker found Rupe Caldwell down at the diggings, watching the repair and rebuilding of his raided and smashed-up sluice boxes. Caldwell's mood was sour and savage and the cold stogie in his lips was chewed to rags. He was ready to rage and curse at anything, which Riker realized, so Riker put it to him, blunt and curt.

"You might as well get a real grip on yourself, Rupe. I got more bad news for you. Bully Girard is dead."

Caldwell swung around. "Dead! Who killed him?"

"Teague. In the Big Nugget. Not half an hour ago."

Caldwell didn't explode. But the stogie, bit cleanly through, fell from his lips. Caldwell spat out the other portion. "How'd it happen?"

Riker shrugged. "Bully was in the side room with his shotgun. Teague was sitting at a poker table, watching Jack Case turn a game of solitaire. Bully came out on the shoot, but Teague was too fast for him. He got out of the way of Bully's first shot, then beat him to the next. He put two more into Bully to make sure. That fellow Teague is rough medicine."

Caldwell went strangely quiet. Then he admitted heavily, "Yes, he's all of that. I knew it when I brought him in here. That's why I wanted him. But how could I have known he would go stiff-necked on me?"

"Your mistake was in jumping all over him because he wasn't able to stop that raid on your sluices," said Riker. "He wasn't at fault. From talk I've heard around town, Barney Foxx had enough miners behind him to have whipped half a regiment. You should have gone a little slow there."

"Maybe," admitted Caldwell. "But it wouldn't have done any good. Teague was set to break with me anyhow. I saw it coming up." Now some of the frustrated venom in him broke through and his tone-harshened. "Damn a blundering fool like Girard! I out-lined the whole play for him. I knew that Teague was bound to show up in the Big Nugget, sooner or later. I knew he'd show there because I know the kind of a man he is. Just proud enough and stiff-necked enough to show in my own place to prove he wasn't afraid. How in hell could Girard have

168

muffed things when he had first bite and with a shotgun full of buckshot, at that? Teague must have the luck of the devil riding with him."

"I wouldn't know anything about the luck angle," drawled Wade Riker. "But I do know that Jim Teague is one tough monkey."

"Afraid of him, are you?" rapped Caldwell with some sarcasm.

Riker's black eyes pinched down slightly. "Maybe — a little. How about you?"

Caldwell did not answer, but a flush deepened the floridness of his face. He kicked a savage toe into the gravel, then swung around and started for town. "Come on," he growled. "We'll have to figure a new angle at getting rid of him."

In the Big Nugget things were very quiet. The body of Bully Girard had been taken away and a swamper had just finished some work with a mop and bucket of water around the threshold of the side room. Rupe Caldwell paused at the bar and rapped a sharp question at the bartender.

"You saw it happen, Frank?"

"I saw it," nodded the bartender. "All of it."

"What did you see?"

The bartender told his story. "All Girard hit," he ended, "was the edge of that poker

169

table yonder. But Teague, he didn't miss at all. There, for my money, is one man who knows a gun from a bung starter. Me, I want no part of him."

"Give me a quart," growled Caldwell.

He carried the bottle into the side room opened it and poured drinks for Riker and himself. His own drink was a plenty heavy one and he took it down in one long gulp. Riker eyed him narrowly.

"Whiskey's whiskey, Rupe — and has its uses. But it strikes me you've been pushing at it pretty heavy lately. I like my share of it, but I'm not blind to what too much of it can do to a man. Better think about that."

Caldwell lighted a fresh stogie. "All I can think of is that damn blunderer of a Girard, messing up his job. With a shotgun, surprise and first bite — and still he muffed it. I tell you, Teague's got the luck of the devil!"

Riker slouched down in his chair, built a cigarette. "Maybe. Maybe it can run out, too. For that matter, maybe ours is running out. Maybe it's time to toss in our cards in this camp, Rupe — to be satisfied with what we've got and light a shuck out of here."

"And leave the fortune that's still in those claims? No!" Caldwell slammed a fist on the table by way of emphasis. "Hell, man — we're just getting into it really rich. Give me another three weeks — a month, and then they can have the damn camp. But I'm not tossing in my cards now."

Wade Riker blew a thin line of blue smoke toward the ceiling. "This is your first gold camp, Rupe. But it's not mine. I've seen several in my time. And I know how things move in them. Things climb to a peak in all of them. Before that peak is reached everybody is too damn busy scratching for gold to think of anything else. But there's always a few solid men in every camp, men like Ben App, Barney Foxx, Tim McCord, Duff Sherrill. They begin to make their influence felt, gather a following. The old instinct for law and order begins to break through. When that happens it's wise business for fellows like you and me to be a long ways away and traveling fast. Well, that peak is just about reached here in Bonanza Gulch."

Caldwell's heavy lips pulled into a snarling grin. "You're the law and order in this camp, Wade. What more do these stupid fools want?"

Riker stirred irritably. "Lousy joking, Rupe. Get it through your head that we're fooling nobody any more."

"You fooled Duff Sherrill enough to get hold of that injunction, didn't you? No, we still got 'em buffaloed."

"Let's not," suggested Riker quietly, "forget friend Teague. You in particular better not forget him."

Caldwell scowled and poured another drink, a big one. "I'll take care of Teague. This time I put George Ides and Curly Bolan on that chore. Those boys really know how to work, in daylight or in dark. They won't louse things up."

"I still say," insisted Riker, "that we'd be smart to call it a day."

Caldwell was feeling the liquor now. It made him feel big, unbeatable. "Wade," he jibed, "you're losing your nerve."

Riker got up, moved around the room, ended up at the door. The glance he laid on Caldwell held a shading of contempt. "The state of my nerves isn't bothering me any," he said cuttingly. "At least I don't get mine out of a bottle. So I'll be around when the big divvy comes. Just remember that, Rupe. I'll be around!"

Wade Riker went out, closed the door behind him. Caldwell stared at the door for a long moment. Then he growled, "Maybe you will, Wade — maybe you will. We'll see."

Rupe Caldwell kept staring at the door and at the moistness of the floor under it. Right there Bully Girard had died, before the gun of Jim Teague. That was a deal, Caldwell thought, that he and Girard had figured out carefully. But it had backfired, and Girard, instead of Jim Teague, was dead. Was it, somehow, indicative of what the future held?

Caldwell poured another drink, gulped it down. Damn Jim Teague! Damn him everlastingly. . . .

Caldwell went over to his safe, opened it and looked over the fat gold pokes stacked up in it. He counted them, tested their solid weight, one by one. His heavy mouth grew loose and a fever began to burn in his eyes. Why, with the wealth these pokes represented and with what was yet to come, he could make the future an empire for himself.

For a long half hour Rupe Caldwell crouched before that safe, dreaming his distorted dreams, while his face worked and changed and worked again under the drive of gross greed. When he finally straightened and closed the safe he weaved a trifle on his feet, as though the fever of the gold had made him drunk.

He went back to the table, shook himself and from a table drawer drew a pack of cards. He still had many plans to make, to think out, and he had found that it always helped his thought processes to turn cards. He shuffled the pack, edged them up neatly and turned the first card for a layout of solitaire. That first card was the ace of spades!

Sight of it brought Rupe Caldwell up with a jerk. He stared at it, shook himself again and started to turn the second card. His fingers slowed, the move stopped, half-formed. It seemed his eyes refused to leave that black ace. A curse broke from him. He sent all the cards to the floor with a savage sweep of his hand and reached for the whiskey bottle.

When the candle went out before the snaky sweep of Curly Bolan's hand, Jim Teague was already moving to the right, away from that open door. For he knew that the instinct of location in men for familiar things was strong. Like the position of a door or a window in a room one knew well. In a cabin as small as this one, a man who had lived in it could throw a shot at either window or door in black darkness and rarely miss.

Teague's life rested on that move and he knew it. For now a spurt of crimson gun flame lanced the cabin's blackness and the very wall shook to the thunder of the report. And the slug ripped through that open door where Teague had stood a moment before.

174

The gun flame licked out, not from the floor where Curly Bolan had thrown himself, but from the far end of the table where the shaggy-headed man had been sitting. Teague drove two shots back, guiding them by that tongue of hostile gun flame. The next moment his feet, still shifting and turning, struck a tangle of gear on the floor and he fell, full length, the blunt horns of a sawbuck pack saddle jabbing against his legs.

He rolled, fighting clear of the tangle and got one knee under him before he sensed, rather than saw, the bulk of a man diving at him. He had no time to shoot, but slapped out with his gun in a warding-off motion. Steel rang on steel and something that stung like the touch of white hot iron drew a line across his wrist. He knew what it was. A knife!

A curse, thin and venomous, spat at him. Teague drew his left fist, lunging. It struck a man's chest, but without much force behind it for he didn't get much leverage into the blow. Yet it gained him a whisper of time, enough to throw himself ahead and to one side.

He heard the muffled thud of the knife as another driving slash missed and sank the thirsty blade deep into the puncheon floor of the cabin. Teague reached over and back, smashing hard with his gun. This time it landed on flesh and got a muffled gasp in answer. Teague chopped down with the gun again and felt a softening resistance sink under the blow. Then he lurched to his feet, ready to fire at the slightest suggestion of movement or sound.

The cabin was still, so still that when a coal snapped on the hearth it seemed like a pistol shot to Teague's taut and straining nerves. He almost drove a shot in return, but caught himself just in time. He found that he was holding his breath and he let it out in a long, sibilant sigh.

The stillness held. There was a warm sliminess seeping across Teague's wrist where the knife had touched. With his left hand he thumbed his pockets for a match, bent, scratched it along the floor and as it sputtered into flame, held it wide at arm's length. It brought no move, or gunfire. But it's feeble flame disclosed the huddled figures of two men on the floor. One lay over by the table. The other, Curly Bolan, was crumpled almost at Teague's feet.

Relaxation ran through Teague in a muscle-easing shiver. He stepped to the table and used the final flame of the match to recover and relight the candle. With this in his left hand and his gun ready in his right, he made swift examination. The shaggy-headed man was done. But Curly Bolan was alive, unconscious. He lay with his bullet-head sagging to one side. Across the base of big neck and slightly to the back lay a long, livid bruise, where the barrel of Teague's gun had landed. Inches in front of Bolan's open and relaxed right hand a knife stood upward, the point sunk far into a rough pine puncheon of the floor.

A gun belt was about Bolan's waist, holding a holstered gun. But it was indicative of Bolan's makeup that under the stress of surprise and desperate emergency, he had made no slightest attempt to go for the gun, but had instead turned to the weapon he knew and liked best — cold steel. Knifemen, mused Teague bleakly, were like that.

Well, maybe it was his good luck that Bolan had gone for his knife instead of a gun. For with a gun, guiding his shots at the flame of Teague's weapon while Teague was taking care of the bushy-headed man, well — this thing could have ended far differently than it had. As it was, even with his knife, he had come close — very close.

Teague reloaded and holstered his gun. In the candlelight he examined the knife wound on his wrist. It was shallow and, while still bleeding, of no great moment. Teague managed a fair bandage with strips torn from a reasonably clean shirt hanging on a wall peg.

There were three bunks, one above the other against the wall beside the window. Teague dragged Curly Bolan over to the lower one, lifted him on it, then tied him hand and foot with more strips of cloth torn from that shirt. The bushy-headed man he rolled against the wall, covering him with a blanket.

Teague went outside for a look around. There was no telling how far the sound of the guns might have carried, or who, if anyone, was close enough to hear them. There was still another man to be accounted for — George Ides. It was logical to surmise that as long as Ides had not been in the cabin with the others, he was already on his way back to, or at Bonanza Gulch. But having come this far successfully, Jim Teague wanted to take no careless chances.

The night was big and lonely and still, except for some movement in the pole corral where horses, stirred up by the shooting, were milling restlessly about. Teague let the impact of the stars and the high keen breath of the mountains wash all through him, and found it was a cleansing thing, driving the dark mists out of him. For that sort of thing, back there in the cabin, didn't do a man a bit of good, even though he came out of it alive and all in one piece. The harshness, the pulled tautness inside him began to soften up and smooth out. So he recovered his rifle and cut straight across the meadow to where he'd left his horse. The animal whickered soft relief. Teague swung astride and rode back to the cabin.

Curly Bolan was beginning to stir, but was not fully conscious yet. Teague made sure Bolan's bonds were secure, then began looking over the gear stacked in the cabin. Two riding saddles were there and also a pair of sawbuck pack saddles, one of which had tripped Teague up. Besides these, wrapped tightly in canvas and tied so with ropes, were four bundles. When Teague tried to stir one of these with a boot toe he found it very solid and heavy.

He untied the rope about one of these, unrolled the canvas covering. Inside was nearly a score of gold pokes of various size and weight, each tagged with the name of the owner. Here beyond doubt was the loot taken from Bob Porter, the treasure messenger, gold pokes being sent out for safe keeping in the bank at Timber Lodge. In these four packs were thousands of dollars in gold dust.

Teague remade the bundle he had opened, resumed his search of the cabin, but found nothing more of importance. An old Sharps rifle stood in one corner and from under the table he retrieved a worn Peacemaker Colt gun which the shaggy-headed man had used in his single try to get Teague. On the walnut butt the initials A. C. were roughly carved. Which meant nothing to Teague and he was about to toss the weapon aside when he realized the initials might mean something to Ben App, back in Bonanza Gulch.

A thin curse came from the bunk where Curly Bolan lay. Teague moved across to him, looked down at the venomous, bullet-headed knifeman.

"You should have tried with your gun, Bolan," Teague told him. "You might have had better luck. But, once a knifeman, always a knifeman, so the old saying goes. Who was your friend who tried, but didn't get there?"

Bolan cursed again.

"What became of your partner in the holdup, George Ides?" asked Teague.

Bolan held to the same answer. Teague shrugged. "You may talk later, Bolan — when the miners put a rope around your neck. We're heading back to Bonanza Gulch — tonight."

Hours later, Jim Teague rode down the Blizzard Pass road into Bonanza Gulch. Behind him four horses followed at lead. Two of these carried pack loads of golden treasure. On a third Curly Bolan sat, humped and venomously silent, wrists tied to the saddle horn, ankles to the cinch rings. Across the saddle of the fourth horse a dead man was jackknifed, a shaggy-headed man with a beaked nose.

On leaving the lonely cabin far back in the Shawmuts, Jim Teague had taken no chances of getting lost in dark and unfamiliar country. He had struck due east, fixing his route by the coldly brilliant stars. He knew that in this way he was bound to strike the road which cut across the Shawmuts by way of Blizzard Pass.

It was well past midnight when he reached the camp, which lay still and sleeping. He pulled around to the rear of the stage station, pounded on the locked door of the place. Presently he raised a stir and then there was Ben App's sleepy voice calling.

"Who is it?"

"Jim Teague."

There was a startled mutter and the door lock snicked. Ben App stuck a tousled head out. "You're back quick, Teague," he growled. "What's the matter — couldn't you pick up that sign you were so sure you could find?"

"I found it," Teague told him succinctly. "Get a light going. I got things to show you."

Ben App scurried about, getting that light and climbing into his clothes. He stared, slack-jawed, as Teague came in, prodding a cursing, surly Curly Bolan ahead of him, wrists tied.

"Watch him!" ordered Teague briefly. "There's more."

Teague brought in the treasure packs, one by one, and they thudded heavily as he dropped them to the floor. "Recognize these, Ben?" he asked.

"I should," gulped Ben App. "I made them up for Bob Porter." There was a slightly awed note in the stage agent's voice. "Teague, I'm eating a lot of things I've said about you."

Teague shrugged. "Forget it. I'll need help with this next one. A dead man. But first, let's make sure Mister Bolan stays with us."

Teague tripped Curly Bolan neatly and held him down while Ben App tied his feet. They rolled him against a wall, went out and brought in a final grim burden. Teague said, "I never saw this one before. Maybe you have?"

Ben App started to shake his head, then looked closer. He straightened and said definitely, "The hair and whiskers nearly fooled me. Yeah, I know him. He was in Bonanza Gulch last fall, but dropped out of sight last winter. A tinhorn gambler, he was known as One Card Dan. That's the only name I ever heard him called. Some of the old-timers might know his full name. How did he get tied up in this affair?"

"I'll tell you the full story later," said Teague. "I wasn't able to locate any sign of George Ides."

"Ides was back on the job as faro lookout in the Big Nugget tonight," Ben App said. "I saw him there myself about nine o'clock."

Teague considered a moment. "He could have managed that easy enough," he decided. "With a good horse under him he could have got back by that time. Probably things had been figured that way, to make them look good. If George Ides was to disappear for any extended length of time, somebody might wonder why and begin asking questions, particularly when word of the holdup got out. On the other hand, Curly Bolan could drop from sight and hardly be missed."

"Something in that, all right," agreed Ben App. "Find anything else of interest?"

Teague started to shake his head, then remembered. "I brought this along." He pulled an old Peacemaker Colt gun from his coat pocket and held it out. "Brought it because of the initials in the butt. Figured it might give a tip as to the identity of the one you just named as One Card Dan. Which don't jibe with the initials, though. They read A. C."

Ben App turned the gun over in his hands, looking at it closely. "Good Lord!" he exclaimed. "You know who used to pack this gun, Jim?"

"I haven't the, faintest idea. All I know is that this One Card Dan hombre had it and made a try at me with it."

"This gun," stated Ben App gravely, "belonged to Andy Carr, the man whose discovery claim started this camp. I'm positive of it. This could mean that when Andy Carr disappeared so suddenly —" Ben App broke off, staring grimly at the body of the man known as One Card Dan.

"Whatever it means," said Jim Teague wearily, "it will keep until daylight. Right now I got some broncs to unsaddle and take care of. And then I could stand a few hours of sleep. How's chances to use a chunk of your floor, Ben?"

"Floor — hell!" sputtered the stout little

stage agent. "You get a bunk in my living quarters. Go turn in. I'll take care of those horses. And I'll take care of friend Bolan, too."

Jim Teague awoke with sunlight pouring in his face through the window above his bunk. He got up and dressed and went out into the main room of the stage station. Here he found Ben App in sober, grim discussion with several other men, all miners. One of these was black-bearded, flaming-eyed Barney Foxx. Also present, gaunt and grizzled and using his rough, homemade cane, was Duff Sherrill.

The talk among these men ceased as Teague came in and the miners eyed him with a grave respect. Teague looked around and said quietly, "Don't let me interrupt, gentlemen. I just wanted to find out if the prisoner is still with us. Then I'm going out to rustle some breakfast."

"The prisoner is just where you left him last night, Jim," said Ben App. "Go get that breakfast and then come back here. These men and I — we want the full story before we decide on a pretty important matter."

"I'll be back," promised Teague.

He ate at the hashhouse and was back in the stage station within half an hour. The miner group stirred restlessly as Teague

185

came in and Barney Foxx cleared his throat.

"Ben, here, tells us that you and Caldwell have had a split up, Teague. How did that come about?"

Teague considered quietly. "Put it that I felt there were angles to the job I didn't like. I hope you believe me this time, Foxx. I told you once before I was done with Caldwell, but you didn't seem to take much stock in it."

Barney Foxx flushed. "You've proven several things since then. You feel that Caldwell set Bully Girard off in that try he made to get you?"

"Yes," nodded Teague, "I do."

"There's no question," went on Barney Foxx, "but that you've done us a mighty big turn in getting back the load of treasure Bob Porter started out with. In case you didn't know it there was right on fifty thousand dollars' worth of gold in those pack loads. The point I'm driving at is, though, how much of that chore did you do in the interest of law and order and common on honesty, and how much merely as a chance to hit back at Caldwell?"

"The issue between me and Caldwell is man to man and I hope to finish it that way," said Teague, a flutter of grimness touching his cheeks. "About this gold, well, I saw a brave man, Bob Porter, come in shot to ribbons. And, while I'm no saint and make no pretensions as such, neither am I a damn thief, nor do I have any use for such. Again, I wanted to square myself in the eyes of the honest men of this camp, and the chance looked right. So that's about how it was. You talk like you're convinced that Caldwell was the mind behind the holdup."

Barney Foxx shrugged. "It was pulled by Caldwell's men. And it ties in with other things he's pulled. It's a pretty strong straw in the wind. And now we're going to do something about it."

"From where I stand, I'd have thought you'd have done something about Rupe Caldwell, long ago," Teague said drily.

Barney Foxx shrugged again. "Not as easy as all that. If we try and act as individuals, that makes things a personal vendetta. And that isn't law and order, which is what we want and what this camp has to have. Up to now the majority of us hadn't been kicked around enough to form a solid front and stay that way. Oh, on the spur of the moment the boys would get worked up over something, like they did when Claus Lehrmann was murdered and robbed. But they cooled off quick, being more interested in their personal fortunes."

"And in the meantime, Rupe Caldwell keeps on getting away with murder, literally," said Teague.

"That," admitted Foxx, "is the way it has been. Caldwell has had a pretty powerful organization working for him. But not all of them are definitely the wrong kind. You take those men who are right now working his sluices for him. Most of them hit this camp as average miners. They found the best of the claims already taken up. Trying to work what was left, they couldn't make wages, or a living. So they had to go looking for a job. Caldwell picked them up, gave them that job, paying them fat wages. So they're with him now and will fight for him. But they're not fundamentally bad men. And they see Caldwell as a pretty regular guy."

"He's a past master at putting on that kind of a front, all right," conceded Teague. "He had me fooled for a while, so I can see why those men feel as they do."

"Exactly!" said Foxx. "So, every time some of us played with the idea of getting together a force to really smash Caldwell, we had to face the fact that a mob can get out of hand. In which case, innocent as well as guilty could suffer. We had to wait around until we had sheer, cold proof against definite individuals. We feel we have that now, and this committee of us are ready to act. But first, we want your story of how you ran down this treasure and what happened when you did. We're listening."

Teague built a cigarette, then told his story, told of how he'd picked up the trail, where it led him to and what happened in that lonely little cabin far back in the Shawmuts. "George Ides left town with Curly Bolan, but he wasn't at the cabin when I got there," Teague ended. "He'd already pulled out and returned to Bonanza Gulch. But he was most certainly in on the holdup. Now, here is something else which you men may never have considered, but which I've done plenty of thinking about."

Teague told this angle briefly. Told of a stage holdup with two men left dead along the Blizzard Pass road. Told of sign which pointed to two men having pulled that crime. Told also of an empty revolver shell, carelessly tossed aside. "That shell," Teague emphasized, "was a .44 Russian, not exactly a common gun in parts like these. Later, I had cause to tangle a little with George Ides, and I took his gun away from him. It was a .44 Russian. Do you men know of any other .44 Russian models in Bonanza Gulch? No? Well, store that fact away in your minds."

Teague let his glance swing over the room,

meeting the eyes of this man and that. They were listening intently, all of them, hanging on his every word. They were the same group who had been here before he went to breakfast, with the exception of one. Duff Sherrill was no longer present, had probably gone back to his cabin to rest.

"Now," went on Teague, "I got another picture I want you to look at. I'm going back to that Claus Lehrmann affair. On a certain night, Claus Lehrmann was stabbed to death in his blankets and robbed of a rich poke. The news of Lehrmann's strike had gone all over camp. Well, on the night Lehrmann was killed, Curly Bolan was one of a shift guarding Caldwell's sluice boxes. But Bolan turned up missing for a full hour. And Bolan is strong for knife work. I know." Teague held up his bandaged wrist.

A long sigh went through the assembled men. Barney Foxx said, "Obliged, Teague. Now this thing gets serious, plenty. Want to sit in on the rest of it?"

Teague knew what Barney Foxx meant. This day, something stark and grim that had long hovered over Bonanza Gulch was due to become actuality. But the finish, as Teague saw it, was none of his affair. That was up to this miners' court. So he shook his head.

"Your ride, gentlemen. I've had my say. Good luck!"

Teague went out and the assembled miners began to stir. Barney Foxx held up his hand to quiet them. "We act today, boys — or we never will," he said gruffly. "Let's review some facts. None of us wants to make a mistake that we'll regret. But something has to be done. You've just heard what Teague had to say. What he told us concerning that stage holdup points a mighty accusing finger. What he told us about the Claus Lehrmann affair does the same thing."

"That's right, Barney, it does," spoke up a miner. "But, while I admit the evidence is strong, it's still only circumstantial, and a pointed finger ain't cold proof. I don't move in this thing until we come to cold proof."

"Of course, Sam," agreed Barney Foxx. "You're absolutely right, there. Cold proof is what we all want. Well, we got it in this last holdup. We know that Bob Porter was robbed, fatally wounded. We know that Jim Teague went out, hit the trail and came up with the treasure. We know who he found with that treasure. Curly Bolan. No court in the world could ask for any more unassailable proof of murder and robbery than that. We can only suspect that Curly Bolan had a hand in the stage robbery, or that he was the

one who knifed and robbed Claus Lehrmann. But we are certain he had a hand in
the killing and robbing of Bob Porter. And
for that crime he deserves to swing. Anybody got anything more to say?"

Ben App spoke with quiet certainty. "If
we considered this thing for a thousand
years, we couldn't arrive at more definite
proof. Barney is right, boys. Curly Bolan
should swing!"

"We'll vote," said Barney Foxx. "My vote
is aye!"

"And mine," said Ben App.

"That goes for me," said a third.

It came over them all at once, this group
of rough, grim men. It came as it had come
to others of their kind in scores of wild
mining camps and frontier settlements before Bonanza Gulch was ever heard of and it
would come in other gold camps long after
Bonanza Gulch had faded only to a
memory. It was the inevitable rebellion of
fundamentally good men against the high
crimes and misdeeds of the fundamentally
bad ones. It was the age-old instinct for law
and order that had struggled up through
mankind over all the ages. It was the instinct
that had enabled men to live together in a
common security. It was one of the basic
cornerstones of civilization itself.

There was no levity in them as they made their dread but necessary decision. Shoulders straightened, heads went back. A certain inscrutable, fearless calmness showed in their eyes. This thing they proposed to do entailed the acceptance of a grim and unwavering responsibility. A responsibility to themselves, to their fellow men and to the judgment of history. In grave solemnity they accepted it.

"The crossbar above my high corral gate will serve, gentlemen ," said Ben App.

Now that their minds were fully made up to it, they moved swiftly and with unrelenting purpose. Curly Bolan was put on a horse and the horse led under the crossbar of the corral gate. The rope was affixed to the bar, noosed about Bolan's neck.

They offered Bolan a chance to talk. The answer was a string of foul, scalding curses.

A quirt slapped the horse and it jumped ahead. The crossbar of the corral gate creaked and creaked again.

VIII

THE STALKING SHADOW

When Jim Teague left the stage station, he went over to lounge in the sun by the trading post. He backed up against the wall of this place and spun a cigarette. He knew full well the grim decision that was being made over in the stage station and he knew how it would come out. Those miners might argue and talk for a while, but the decision was already made for them. Here was the turning point in the affairs of Bonanza Gulch. If the miners did not act now, then they never would; if they were not convinced now, then they never would be. But they would act.

Well, he'd done his part. Any debt he'd owed the better element of Bonanza Gulch, he'd now paid. He had saved the miners a fortune in gold. He'd brought in two culprits, one dead, the other alive. And he'd pointed the trail to others of the same stripe. Nobody could rightly ask more of him.

The old, complete sense of physical well-being, of supreme fitness was once more his, and with it had come a cold and daring reck-lessness. Owing this camp nothing more at all, he had no more real interest in it, for it wasn't his kind of country and the people in it, for the most part, were not his kind of people. He could leave the place at any time now, his conscience completely clear. But Rupe Caldwell had set a human gorilla in the form of Bully Girard after him with a sawed-off shotgun and Caldwell had made his threats. Thereby, Caldwell had bought himself a fight. So Jim Teague was sticking around now for the final finish.

To some men, danger is a stimulant. It was so now with Jim Teague. He knew without question that every moment he stayed in Bonanza Gulch from now on, he carried his life in his hand. But the reckless-ness in him liked the spice of the thought. He thumped a fist against his completely healed side and could not raise a twinge. He had washed and fixed a fresh bandage about the knife cut on his wrist and it felt all right. Yeah, he was ready for anything.

Only once did something come into his eyes to shadow the cold alert gleam of them. That was when he looked down across town to the Sherrill cabin. For a short time, into a life that had known little of her kind, a slim and lovely girl had entered. But just as abruptly she had moved out again. Teague shook himself.

It was, he mused grimly, just as well. For what had he to offer a girl like Janet Sherrill? At best he was just an ordinary cattle hand, knowing the cattle trade well, but possessing nothing beyond that knowledge. At worst he was a man with a ready and lightning-fast gun, with a future that was a day-by-day gamble, and a past that had left him with no material substance at all. These were brief and fragile things indeed to offer any woman.

Teague swung his glance along the street and saw Sheriff Wade Riker come out of the Big Nugget. Riker stood for a little time in front of the place, idle eyes running. It reached Teague and settled there. Then Riker swung out into the street and came angling across it, straight for Teague, who drew a final deep inhale on his cigarette, then tossed the butt aside and waited with a fine fixed wariness.

There was no visible hostility, save perhaps a glint in his cold black eyes, about Wade Riker as he came up. He nodded briefly.

"Surprises me to see you here, Teague. Yesterday you were seen riding out of camp and the guess was that you'd decided to shake out of Bonanza Gulch for good."

"Bum guess," said Teague tersely. "Tell Caldwell he don't get off that easy."

"Really got your roach up for Rupe, eh?"

"He's asked for it."

Riker's black eyes pinched down slightly and he spoke with slow distinctness. "Girard was a slow-witted, clumsy fool. Others may not be."

"Meaning you, maybe?" There was a rough and thrusting challenge in Teague's tone. He was not giving an inch.

A shade of color swept Riker's dark face. "Don't get too proud, Teague. Where did you ride yesterday?"

"Does it matter? I'm here, now!" Again there was that thrusting challenge.

Their eyes locked, frigid gray against veiled black. Riker shrugged and turned away. But as he went he threw a parting remark over his shoulder. "Stubborn fools die young, Teague."

Teague smiled mirthlessly. Words never killed any man.

Duff Sherrill, grizzled and gaunt, using his cane, came limping over from his cabin. Riker made as if to pay him no attention, but Sherrill headed Riker off, calling to him. Riker shrugged irritably, then swung around and waited while Sherrill came shuffling up. Jim Teague heard Sherrill's question plainly.

"When are you going to serve that injunction, Riker? Rupe Caldwell's got those sluices runnin' again and every minute you allow that to go on means dollars that Caldwell is robbin' me of. Get busy and serve that paper!"

Wade Riker's reply was mockingly thin. "What are you talking about, Sherrill? I don't know anything about an injunction."

Jim Teague saw Duff Sherrill's chin drop, saw his face twist and congest with a furious anger. His words were almost a shout.

"You know damn well what I'm talking about, Riker. And you know all about that injunction. I gave it to you with my own hand."

"You're losing your mind, Sherrill," Riker jeered. "I tell you I don't know anything about an injunction and I don't want to." With that he turned and walked away.

Shaking with a helpless anger, Duff Sherrill stared after him. Then the gaunt, grizzled old fellow's thin shoulders sagged and he weaved unsteadily. A slim figure darted out of the Sherrill cabin and came running. Janet Sherrill hurried up to her father, put a steadying arm about him.

"What is it, Dad?" she cried. "What did Wade Riker say?"

The old miner's voice sounded hollow and beaten. "I've been a fool, daughter. I should have listened to that fellow, Teague. He told us that if we let Riker get his hands on that injunction, we'd never see it again. Riker just said he didn't know anything about such an injunction. He was sneering, laughing at me. Yeah, I've been a driveling old fool. This looks like the end of things for us, child."

Jim Teague wished he was further away, wished he did not have to listen to this, or watch it. And he would have moved away had not the girl whirled and come hurrying up to him. Her eyes were flashing through tears.

"I — I suppose you're laughing at us, too!" she charged. "Because we wouldn't listen to you — because we've been fools. I suppose that amuses you — you — ?" She broke off, her voice thickening in her throat.

Teague answered her gravely. "Of course I'm not amused, or laughing at you. That isn't being very kind, Janet Sherrill, saying such things. For I don't believe I've ever given you any reason to believe I'd ever laugh at you or be amused over your misfortune. I'm truly sorry."

He started to turn away, but her hand fell on his arm. "Wait — please!" She was trying to work the stricture out of her throat. She managed to finally. "I didn't mean that —

really I didn't. It's just that everything has gone so wrong I don't know which way to turn. The law — Dad and I thought surely the law would protect us."

"Real law would," said Teague. "But there is no such law in Bonanza Gulch at present. Wade Riker may pose as the law, but it's just a pose. He's Rupe Caldwell's man and he does what Caldwell tells him to do."

She was looking at him steadily and Jim Teague thought he'd never seen anything so llovely as her eyes washed with tears. Now she spoke simply.

"I have no right in the world to ask this of you, Jim Teague. But you're the only one in this camp I can turn to. And isn't there some way in this that you could help us? I'm not asking it for myself. I'm asking it for my father. He's old and tired. This claim, the one Caldwell has stolen from him, why, that's the claim he's been searching for all his life. It means so much to him. And now, if he loses it, I'm afraid he'll never leave Bonanza Gulch alive. I — I hope you understand —"

"Yes," said Teague, almost gently, "I understand. I'll do what I can. Now you take your father back to your cabin and keep him there. And until I tell you different, don't you trust a single soul in this camp but your father, yourself and me. Make your father understand that, too. He mustn't discuss his future plans with a single soul but you or me."

She was startled at the intentness of Teague's final words, sensing some hidden meaning behind them. She said, "Les Jardeen comes to see father regularly. They talk of —"

"In particular, don't trust Les Jardeen," broke in Teague. "You'll have to promise me that, if you want me to help in this thing. Remember, I was right about that injunction. I'm right about Les Jardeen."

She stared at him fixedly for a long moment. Then she nodded. "Very well. Not a word for anyone but you and Dad and myself. And — thank you, Jim Teague."

It seemed the most natural thing in the world that her hands should come out and rest for a moment in his. Teague smiled down at her. "This town could be in for several wicked, savage days. Reserve judgment on everything until you know all the truth, all the facts. Else you'll end up hating me, probably, Janet Sherrill. Now run along. And if, within the next hour or so you hear a growl like that of a mad animal run all through the camp, stay inside and don't look out. Promise?"

"I promise." Her eyes were very wide and sober. "You hint of something happening that is pretty terrible."

"Of something completely justified, but never pretty," Teague told her.

She hesitated just a moment longer, her fingers tightening about his. "You'll be very careful? If something happened to you, I don't know — I don't know — !"

"I'll be careful," Teague assured her. "Habit of mine. I'll make out. Now, run along."

She scurried away to her father and steered the old fellow's faltering steps toward their cabin. Teague watched until the cabin door closed behind them. And it was right after that that he saw the miners' court come out of the stage station and saw what they intended to do. . . .

A strange and brittle stillness hung over this boom camp of Bonanza Gulch. The word had spread rapidly. Vigilantes had struck. The execution of Curly Bolan was over and done with. Not many had witnessed it. The vigilantes had moved quietly, swiftly and with direct purpose. Down along the diggings as the word reached them, miners ceased their feverish toiling for a little while, to gather in groups and discuss it.

There were some who argued that this thing should have been made more public, taken place before more people, so that it would have emphasized the fact that it met with the approval of all the miners. But there were cannier heads to point out that such a course might have given Rupe Caldwell and his crowd a chance to build up opposition, even thwart the court of justice. These claimed it was a good job, well done and long overdue. And it had been handled with such swiftness and sureness it was certain to throw cold fear into others of Curly Bolan's stripe. It was the swiftness and certainty of punishment, claimed one bearded miner, not the threat of it, that counted.

A few of the hotter-headed advanced the idea that this would be a good time to start a general mob action, to clean up every doubtful person in camp, but this talk was swiftly shouted down. In the end, the more they thought of it, the more the general run of the miners put their full approval behind the action of the vigilante few. It had to come, they agreed, something of this sort. It was history repeating itself. The outlaw element, it seemed, never learned except the hard way. Well, they'd had another lesson.

Despite all the talk and rumor across the diggings, no one seemed to know all the exact details of the affair, so a number of the more curious miners came trooping up to town to gather about the stage station and ask their questions. Jim Teague avoided these men, leaving it up to Ben App and Barney Foxx to enlighten them.

Teague stood quietly apart, watching the street. By this time he knew that the word of what had happened and how, had reached the Big Nugget, and he was guessing about the reaction there. Of one thing he could be very sure. When Caldwell and his cronies got the word that it had been Jim Teague who had trailed down and captured Curly Bolan, and recovered the stolen treasure, they'd be clamoring for his scalp. From here on out, Teague realized, deadly danger would be stalking at his shoulder every moment of the day and night. His life would ride on his unending alertness and the speed of his gun.

When a full hour brought no visible reaction from the Caldwell crowd, Teague went down to the Sherrill cabin. Les Jardeen was just leaving the place, his face clouded and angry. At sight of Teague he made as if to stop, then started on again. Teague called to him.

"Just a minute, Jardeen!"

Jardeen turned, taut and on the defensive.

A flicker of uneasiness lay far back in his eyes as Teague's glance bored at him coldly. Teague's words were as blunt as his manner.

"The vigilante group will probably act on the idea that an accessory to a crime is just as much deserving of the rope as the man or men who actually commit the crime. If that could possibly mean anything to you, Jardeen, you'd be wise to act accordingly."

"I don't know what you mean," retorted Jardeen sullenly.

Jim Teague whipped his open hand across in front of him with a gesture of contempt and thinning patience.

"You did a good man some service when he was down and out, Jardeen. I'm referring to Duff Sherrill. I know that you did this, not out of the goodness of your heart, but because it placed you in a position where you could do some spying. But I'm forgetting that part of it and remembering only that you did make a few days easier for him. But it was hypocritical stuff, Jardeen. It took a particularly low type of human snake to play that kind of a game. As it is, now that I've warned you, I consider that any debt. Duff Sherrill owed you is paid in full. From here on out you'll answer strictly for all future acts. The road over Blizzard Pass is open now. It may not be later — for you!"

Jardeen hung on to some bluster. "You still don't make sense to me, Teague."

Teague's laugh was short and without mirth. "Your kind are all the same, Jardeen. You fancy yourselves as being so slickery and smart that nobody ever sees through you. All right, chew on this. Plans were made in secret among four men to send out a gold messenger over an isolated trail. Along that trail the messenger is held up, shot to pieces, the treasure stolen. There was only one way that George Ides and Curly Bolan could have learned of that treasure shipment. Some one of those four men gave out the word. Ben App, Barney Foxx and Tim McCord didn't. Who does that leave, Jardeen?"

The bluster in Jardeen died completely out. He backed away, licking his lips. He whirled and nearly ran.

Teague went on to the cabin door and knocked. Janet Sherrill opened it. She was pale and still of face, her eyes big and dark with inner strain.

"I saw you coming down here and I held the door open a little," she confessed. "I heard what you said — to Les Jardeen. Is that true?"

Teague looked down at her gravely. "I'm

afraid it is. Sorry you had to hear it."

"You — they — just hung a man — a Curly Bolan?" Her words came out in little gusts of feeling. Teague couldn't tell whether it was accusation he read in her eyes, or aversion, or just plain shock.

"That's right," admitted Teague. "There may be others. It had to come. Something like it has been in the air for days. It's an old story in camps like this one, and the only weapon the decent element in a camp has against the other sort. Don't let it worry you. Curly Bolan was worse than a mad dog running loose."

"I'm not used to things — like that," she said. "I must try and understand. You wanted to see father?"

"If I could," nodded Teague. "Some things I'd like to ask him."

Duff Sherrill sat on a chair in a corner of the cabin, gaunt and thin, head sunk low in dejection. Teague moved over beside him.

"Mr. Sherrill, I understand that you were one of the very first to hit this camp after Andy Carr made the original discovery. That's right, isn't it?"

Duff Sherrill nodded. "Me and Jack Dorgan. I filed on number one below Discovery and Dorgan on number one above. Now Dorgan is dead and I might as well be, for Caldwell is robbing me of dollars in gold every time the clock ticks."

"How about Andy Carr?" asked Teague. "You must have known him well. Did you have any idea that he would ever sell Discovery to Rupe Caldwell?"

Duff Sherrill's grizzled head came up and the hollow boom of his voice took on a firmer, harsher note.

"I don't believe Andy ever did sell. I never have believed it. I'd been talking with Andy only the day before he disappeared. He was telling me all about the plans he had for developing Discovery when spring came and winter began loosening up. He was plenty enthusiastic about it. He never gave even the slightest hint that he expected to sell out to anybody. Why should he have wanted to sell? He'd been looking all his life for a rich strike. He finally found it — here. Does it make sense that he'd sell? No!"

"I understand that Caldwell had a bill of sale for proof," Teague said.

Duff Sherrill snorted. "Anybody could have written that. Nobody I know had ever seen Andy Carr's handwriting. For that matter, I don't know whether Andy could even write at all. Neither does anyone else. Even if he could, I still don't believe Andy ever sold his claim of his own free will."

"In other words," suggested Teague, "you believe that Rupe Caldwell got hold of Discovery by pulling some kind of fast deal?"

"That's exactly what I've always believed. And I've said so, all along. Which is one of the reasons I got a knife stuck into me while I was on my way home to this very cabin one dark night. That, and because I owned number one below Discovery."

Teague built a cigarette. "Andy Carr just simply disappeared between dark and dawn, is that it?"

"That's it," growled Sherrill. "His burros, gear — everything. Which is something else that don't add up. Andy had a lot of friends in this camp. He was the kind of feller who liked people and was fond of his friends, the kind who'd do anything in the world for you if he liked you, and he liked most people. If Andy had left of his own free will, he'd have been around to say goodbye to his friends. But no — pouf! — he was gone, just like that. So I say that Andy Carr's bones are laying out in the mountains somewhere, just like those of other poor devils who got in the way of Rupe Caldwell's crookedness and greed. Andy's cabin was the one that Caldwell now uses for himself."

"How did it happen that both you and Dorgan made a mistake in measurements on location of your claims?" Teague's face was bleak and frowning.

Duff Sherrill looked up at Teague from under shaggy brows. "We didn't. Jack Dorgan and me were old hands at this game. We knew as much as any two men alive about the rules and laws concerning claim locations. We knew we had something good so we were doubly careful about our measurements. But what did Caldwell do? Well, he moved Andy Carr's original discovery stake. And naturally that made it look like mine and Dorgan's measurements were way off."

"Ah!" murmured Teague. "As simple as that, eh?"

Duff Sherrill nodded. "Aye! As simple as that. And it's on that crooked basis that Caldwell jumped our claims. Now Jack Dorgan is dead because he tried to play a lone, tough hand. I'd have probably tried the same if I hadn't been laid up. No question but that Caldwell was somewhere behind that knife in my back. He wanted me dead, too. But when his knifeman wasn't quite expert enough to do a clean job on me, Caldwell probably figured it didn't matter. I was down on my back and out of the way and he could go ahead and loot my claim. You think that maybe that Bolan hombre —

the one the boys just stretched — he was the one who knifed me?"

Teague nodded gravely. "Probably. He was strong for that kind of work."

Duff Sherrill brooded for a moment, then went on. "Laying on my bunk, half-dead, I did a heap of thinking and I realized that I had to have another angle to fight Caldwell if I hoped to save anything out of my claim. So I sent out word to Janet to get a court injunction calling on Caldwell to desist all work on my claim until things could be thrashed out legally. I expected Janet would mail the injunction in to me. Instead, she brought it in personally. Little good it's done me. With my own hands I gave it to that crooked whelp of a Wade Riker to serve. Now he denies ever seeing it. You were right about that angle, Teague. I've been a damn, bungling fool!"

The old miner's head went down again, his shoulders sagged in hopeless despond. The girl moved over to him and put an arm across the gaunt shoulders. "Never mind, Dad," she said. "We'll make out."

Jim Teague stirred, moved toward the door. The girl, looking at him, saw something in his face that brought a sharp dart of alarm into her eyes. "Where are you going?"

"To get that injunction, if it hasn't been

211

destroyed. Once I get it, the vigilante committee will serve it."

There was no need to tell her of the deadly risk this quiet decision entailed. She left her father's side and darted over to Teague as he reached the door.

"No!" she cried. "You mustn't. You owe us nothing, Jim Teague. I won't have you doing this — for us — !"

Teague looked down at her gravely, and what he saw in her eyes made the hard lines of his face break slightly.

"Maybe I owe you more than you think. There was a time when my sense of values was pretty badly mixed. A combination of things got me straightened out, in time. Knowing you was a big part of that combination. Without that, I might have been little better than Rupe Caldwell. So it is I who owe you so much, not the other way around. Don't worry about me. In my way I can be pretty rough when I have to. And," he added drily, "Caldwell and his crowd have found that out."

Teague stepped through and closed the door behind him. He headed uptown and now it was Jack Case who came swiftly across the street to meet him.

"Man — you sure lit a fire under things when you brought in Curly Bolan and got him stretched, Jim!" Case exclaimed. "Now Rupe Caldwell is losing men by the minute. Tappan and Sharpe are pulling out. They want me to go with them. Maybe they're right."

Teague shook his head. "No need of them going, or you either, Jack. You boys have committed no crimes."

"Hah! Maybe not. But try and tell these wild-eyed miners that. We've worked for Caldwell, and that's enough for them. Bolan's lynching has given a lot of them ideas. They go mob-crazy, they're not going to be very particular who they string up, and they won't mess around arguing fine points of what makes guilt and what doesn't."

"There'll be no mob action," Teague declared. "There might have been if the vigilante group hadn't acted on Bolan. Now that the miners see that the vigilante group really mean business, they'll stand back and let the group handle things. Nobody will be hanged who doesn't deserve to be."

"There's a look about you," said Case. "Where are you going?"

Teague told him, briefly. Case whistled softly. "Right into the snake's den, eh? Think that's smart, Jim — to go it alone?"

Teague hitched his shoulders slightly. "They won't be too tough. Not in the open, anyway. That one little touch of vigilante action will take the starch out of most of them. I'll see you later."

"No!" said Jack Case bluntly. "You'll see me now. I'm going along. You'll need someone to watch your back."

"Not your pie, Jack," argued Teague. "You don't owe me anything."

"Wrong!" differed Jack Case stoutly. "I owe you a skin that will still hold water. If you hadn't knocked me out of line with that table in the Big Nugget and then went to work on Bully Girard the way you did, Girard couldn't have missed getting me with part of that spray of buckshot. But that's only half of it. Once or twice in my life I've bumped into men I liked. And — well, let's get going!"

Teague still hesitated. "You got a gun?"

Case nodded. "I got a gun. And in my way I'm not too bad with it."

They went along the street to the Big Nugget and pushed through the door, pausing there for a moment for a careful survey of the room and all it held. There was a scattering of miners present and at a far poker table the dark-eyed dance hall girl sat, listening to something Les Jardeen was saying. To Teague's eyes the girl looked pale and drawn, and seemed to be resisting some argument of Jardeen's.

Burnley, the ugly, dwarfish little piano player, was hunched over the keyboard of the instrument, his stubby fingers wringing out some of that strange and ominous music which seemed all jangling discords, yet held to a pattern that gave it form and substance. Torment was in that music, and a human sentiment that was writhing and restless and sullen. It added to the dry, taut tension which laid an invisible shadow over the entire room.

Jack Case, standing at Teague's elbow, murmured. "That guy Burnley! He gets something out of that cussed piano that gives me the cold creeps."

There was no playing going on at the faro layout, but Ad Forsythe, the tinhorn, sat in his usual place, sliding cards from the box, setting them up in a practice layout. He was doing this mechanically and his flashing fingers were a little hard with the cards, snapping them sharply. The tinhorn, thought Teague sardonically, was seeing the shadow of Curly Bolan, swinging — swinging. . . .

Wade Riker stood at the far end of the bar, brooding over a drink. And of great interest to Teague, the door of the side room was open and, from where he stood, the room appeared to be empty.

Jack Case gave soft murmur again. "Didn't I tell you that you'd raised hell and put a rock under it, Jim? This place is full of ghosts, all ready to fly."

Teague moved along the bar to Wade Riker and the man's head swung and his black eyes watched Teague warily.

"Caldwell around?" Teague asked curtly.

Riker shrugged and shook his head.

Teague said, "Take a look in that side room, Jack."

Case did so, warily first, then stepping boldly through the door. He came out, hand spread upward and empty. He shrugged expressively.

"Where is he, Riker?" demanded Teague.

"Don't know," came the growling answer. "Was wondering about that, myself."

Somehow Teague knew that Riker was telling the truth. He tried another angle. "Duff Sherrill gave you an injunction to serve and enforce, Riker. You've done neither and now you're mocking Sherrill about it, saying you never saw such a paper. That don't go with me. I want that injunction. Where is it?"

Now Wade Riker came up, fully straight, turning a little from the bar, so that he faced Teague fully. His black eyes were cold and unreadable. He said a strange thing. "I'm not one damn bit afraid of you, Teague, though I admit you're as tough a man as I've ever met. But I'm not afraid. I think you realize that. Do you?"

Teague nodded slowly. "Say that I do. It works the other way around, too. And I still want that injunction!"

"A couple of days ago I'd have seen you in hell before giving it to you," stated Riker flatly. "But since then things have happened, and I'm not referring to the lynching of Curly Bolan, either. But nobody can double-cross me and get away with it. That takes in Mister Rupe Caldwell. Here's the injunction. I hope it does you some good."

Riker drew a folded paper from his inside coat pocket and handed it to Jim Teague. Then he downed his drink with a gulp, wiped his lips with the back of his hand, stepped around Teague and Jack Case and walked out of the Big Nugget.

Jack Case let out a long, slow breath. "I will be damned! Now wouldn't that spur you? Just what's bitin' that hombre?"

Jim Teague glanced over the paper Riker had given him, nodded, pocketed it carefully. He turned to the bartender. "Where's Caldwell?"

The bartender shrugged. "Don't know?"

"Sure of that?" Teague's tone held a crackle in it.

"Sure of it."

Teague walked over to the faro layout. Ad Forsythe stirred uneasily. "How about you?" Teague demanded. "You know where Caldwell is?"

"No," said Forsythe. "Haven't any idea."

"How about George Ides?" probed Teague.

"The same goes for Ides," answered the tinhorn. "Things are coming apart at the seams around here."

Teague threw another long, careful look over the place. Les Jardeen and the dark-eyed dance hall girl were still at the poker table, and Burnley, still wringing those weird discords from his piano, was watching them with sullen eyes. Under Teague's glance, Les Jardeen shifted restlessly, met his eyes for one swift moment, then bent all his attention to his companion again.

Teague said, "Come on, Jack." And left the place.

In the street Case asked, "What do you make of Riker, Jim? He sure had something weighty on his mind. You think maybe, that him and Caldwell have split up?"

"Could be. Sounded like it. Well, that's the way it always goes with a setup like Caldwell had put together. Greed brings that particular breed together to start with, and greed breaks them up. You just can't build a sound apple around a rotten core."

"Maybe Caldwell and George Ides have flew the coop," Case hazarded.

"Maybe, but I don't think so. Not yet, anyhow. None of that crowd knew anything about us having Curly Bolan until today. Last night Ides was on duty at the faro layout. Ben App saw him there. And until today, after the word of Bolan's execution got around, Caldwell would have no reason to believe that time was so short and running out on him. There were bound to be a lot of loose ends he hadn't had time to tie together, plans still on the fire. My guess is that Caldwell will try to take care of some of those things before he lights out. He still has that crew of men working those sluice boxes and there's bound to be a lot of gold racked up in them. Caldwell would want to collect that. No, I don't believe he's pulled stakes just yet."

"What are you going to do now?" Case asked.

"Serve this injunction and run Caldwell's crowd off Duff Sherrill's claim. You stick around town and keep an eye on things, Jack. If Caldwell shows up, or if you happen to pick up any real word about him, let me know right away."

"That," agreed Case, "I'll do." His glance

ran up and down the street. "Ghosts," he murmured, "getting ready to fly. Jim, I'm glad I've never had any yearning to climb into boots too big for me."

IX

WHEN THIEVES FALL OUT

When Jim Teague went into the stage station he found Ben App with an item of news. "Finally found a miner who knew a little something about that fellow One Card Dan that you caught in that cabin with Curly Bolan. One Card Dan's last name was Ormond. Does that mean anything to you, Jim?"

Teague shook his head. "Not the slightest."

"He was," said Ben App sententiously, "a brother of Judge Ormond of Timber Lodge."

"There's been black sheep in the best of families," said Teague.

"I'm wondering," mused App, his eyes pinched with thought. "The kind of setup that Rupe Caldwell had in this camp isn't something that you just throw together. It was too well laid out for that. It must have been pretty carefully figured out beforehand, with allowance made for any angle that might crop up. And — there's been venal judges before this."

Teague drew the injunction from his pocket, tapped it with a forefinger. "But Judge Ormond of Timber Lodge signed this injunction."

Ben App exclaimed. "Let me see that!"

He glanced over it, then stared at Teague soberly. "Duff Sherrill told me the story about this paper. Now how in hell did you get it away from Wade Riker? Jim, you must be a damned magician. Why this paper could represent a fortune, either way. How did you get it?"

Teague grinned slightly. "Just asked Riker for it and he handed it over."

"Wade Riker," declared Ben App bluntly, "is a damned crooked scoundrel. But the man is game. There's no saffron in him. You must have made that request mighty emphatic."

"I was prepared to if I had to," admitted Teague. "But something was on Riker's mind. He made some talk about not standing for a double-cross from anyone. He was obviously sore at Caldwell about something. So he gave me the injunction. That's all there was to it, Ben."

"You make it sound simple," grunted the stage agent. "Main point is, you got it."

"Yeah, I got it. But I don't get your angle about this Judge Ormond business. If he was tangled up with Caldwell, like you suggest he might be, he wouldn't have signed that injunction to hit against Caldwell, would he?"

"Why not?" said Ben App. "Judge Ormond was the one who sent Wade Riker in to represent the law in this camp. Riker, in other words, is Ormond's own hand-picked man. So, while issuing the injunction is one thing, getting it served is something else. My guess is that when Judge Ormond issued this paper he knew it wouldn't be served. Riker would see to that. But the issuing of it would make the judge look good. After all, he couldn't have refused outright to issue the injunction without putting himself in a pretty queer spot. So he played a case game."

"That," admitted Teague, "makes sense. I'd sure like to know what it is that's turned Wade Riker sore at Caldwell."

Ben App shrugged. "What's the old saying about there being no honor among thieves? Plenty of truth in that, Jim. The wrong kind get along fine together as long as everything runs smooth and sweet their way. But when the trail begins to get rocky and things start coming apart, why then it's every man for himself and the old double-cross gets worked overtime. Well, now we got this injunction, what do we do with it?"

"Serve it," rapped Teague. "The same group who hung Curly Bolan — your vigilante group. You've made a good start toward law and order. Here's the next opportunity to show you mean business."

Ben App nodded slowly. "As good an idea as any. We'll get about it."

The vigilante group had, by this time, scattered to go about their own personal affairs and it took some time to round them up and explain matters to them. But once they understood, they were swift to act. In a grim-faced group they moved down on number one below Discovery.

The men at work there laid aside their picks and shovels and reached for rifles as the miners approached. A spokesman for the sluice gang swung his weapon menacingly.

"Keep off! Nobody comes on this claim without direct orders from Rupe Caldwell. Keep wide!"

Jim Teague had given the injunction to Barney Foxx, who now stepped out ahead. Barney knew the leader of the sluice gang by name and now he said, "Before you get your roach up too high, Means, you better take a look at this."

Jake Means accepted the injunction, read

it slowly. He shrugged and spat. "Don't mean a thing unless it's served by an accredited lawman, Foxx."

Foxx waved a hand indicating the group with him. "Look 'em over, Means. You must have heard about Curly Bolan. Well, these are the men who hung him."

Jake Means' eyes flickered. "Yeah? What's that got to do with it?"

"Considerable. We've decided to bring some real law to this camp. Most of the miners along the diggings are satisfied to have it that way. We can send out a call and have a hundred of them to back our hand at any time. Now, if you want to try and shoot it out against those kind of odds, that's your privilege. But do you think it would do you any good? Look, Means — so far you and these others with you have done nothing worse than work for Rupe Caldwell and take his wages. Nobody holds that against you, particularly. But if you once start swapping lead with decent men in Caldwell's interest, then you've put yourself in Curly Bolan's class and can expect no more consideration than he got. You got five minutes to make up your minds. Get your gang together and figure out your answer."

Jake Means scowled, then shrugged. "I'll see what the boys think."

He called his group to one side and explained matters to them. Almost immediately four of them laid down their tools and guns, gathered up their coats and other personal gear and were ready to leave.

"I've worked for Rupe Caldwell," one of them declared with emphasis. "But damned if I want to get my neck stretched for him. As far as I'm concerned, that injunction means everything it says."

The remaining four were hesitant, still a little stubborn. Jake Means turned to Barney Foxx. "We'll leave, but first we clean up the sluices. The gold in them belongs to Rupe Caldwell."

Barney Foxx shook his head. "Jake, you're a good man and an honest one. But that gold don't belong to Caldwell. It belongs to the man who rightfully owns this claim — Duff Sherrill. Caldwell has stolen all the gold he's going to in this camp."

Jake Means scowled, held his ground. But one of the other's spoke up.

"How do we know what's right or wrong, Foxx? Maybe that injunction is legal, maybe it ain't. Where's the proof to show that Rupe Caldwell doesn't actually own this claim?"

"Duff Sherrill," explained Foxx patiently, "asked that this injunction be drawn up. Which shows he's ready and willing to let a court of law decide who rightfully owns the claim. Is Caldwell willing to do that? No! He's out to try and strip the claim before any court has a chance to act. That ought to prove to you who actually owns the claim."

To this another of the sluice gang nodded. "That makes sense. All we can believe in is that injunction. Looks legal and right to me. If Caldwell wants to argue this, let him do it personal. Jake, we ain't got a chance. Let's be smart about this."

That decided it. Jake Means and his men cleared out, tramped back toward town. Ben App let out a sigh of relief.

"They're not bad fellows. I'm glad we didn't have to get rough with them. Caldwell's been the cause of enough blood spilled in this camp."

"There may be more spilled before he's done," prophesied Barney Foxx. "What about the gold in the sluices, Ben?"

Jim Teague spoke up. "How about making a cleanup right now? And taking the stuff to Duff Sherrill. I had a talk with him today. He's plenty low. But I think if he had the cleanup from the sluices stacked in a corner of his cabin, it would do a lot toward making him a well man again. Barney, you know how to go about such things. Let's do it and give Sherrill a pleasant surprise."

"Why, now," agreed Barney, "I can't think of a better idea. Let's get at it."

They cut the water from the sluices, then carefully sacked the concentrate caught behind the riffle cleats. The afternoon was pretty well run out by the time they were done. While Ben App and some of the others lugged the sacks away to Duff Sherrill's cabin, Barney Foxx drew Jim Teague aside.

"What about this fellow Les Jardeen? Ben App's been telling me how you figured that it was Jardeen who tipped off Caldwell about Bob Porter heading out with that load of treasure. If that's true — and it must be, for it's the only way Caldwell could have heard about it, then Jardeen deserves exactly what Curly Bolan got and what George Ides and Caldwell will get, once we get our hands on them."

Teague built a cigarette. "There's two ways you clean up a place, Barney. The really bad ones you handle with a rope or a gun slug. The weakly crooked ones you run out. There's a difference between the two. Jardeen belongs to the weak class. I've already told him to pull out. Whether he has or not just yet, I don't know. But I'll check up on it. It's hardly a pleasure to hang a man, or smoke him down, either, no matter how much he deserves it, even though it is something that must be done now and then."

Barney Foxx's fierce blue eyes flamed. "Maybe you're right. But when I think about men like Jack Dorgan and Claus Lehrmann, about that stage driver and his shotgun guard, about Bob Porter — all slaughtered by Caldwell and his damned gang, why then I turn pretty damn fundamental. And for anyone who had a hand in any way in sending those good men to their deaths, I vote for the rope, with no favorites played. That takes in Jardeen."

"We'll see," said Teague quietly. "Right now I'm mainly interested in trying to locate Caldwell and George Ides. They weren't at the Big Nugget, or at the cabins or anywhere else around town that I could see. And they weren't down here at the diggings."

"Probably pulled out," growled Barney Foxx. "Run like the damned rats they are, soon as they heard about Bolan. I'm beginning to believe we should have rounded them up before they knew what was in the wind and hung them right alongside of Bolan. In fact, I've been in favor of something like that for weeks. But Ben App, he's so cussed set on being absolutely sure, and having ironbound proof before taking a step."

"Ben's right in that," defended Teague. "Nothing worse than going hog wild and making a mistake that takes the life of an innocent man. You wouldn't want that on your mind, Barney — and I know I wouldn't."

Barney Foxx grunted. "Nothing innocent about Ides or Caldwell that I know of."

"A week ago you'd have been in favor of lynching me," pointed out Teague. "In your eyes then I was as bad as the rest, wasn't I?"

"Yeah," agreed Foxx a trifle sheepishly. "You were. I guess Ben App's right, at that."

"Sure he is. A mighty sound, level-headed man, Ben App. You follow Ben's thinking and you'll never go wrong, Barney. Well, I'll go now and check up on Jardeen."

Jim Teague understood Barney Foxx's sentiments fully and could sympathize with them. When a man's rights had been kicked around, when he'd seen other good men and friends foully done to death and callous robbery take place, to know a deep, ferocious resentment was only natural and human. But true justice was never a wild and rampant thing, hitting indiscriminately. True justice moved precisely and with dignity.

Teague knew not the slightest shred of

personal consideration for Les Jardeen. In a way, Jardeen was even more contemptible than Curly Bolan or any of the others. Bolan had never made any pretense at being anything other than what he actually was, a treacherous, vicious killer. But Les Jardeen had played the part of an honest, decent sort for the single reason of being able to spy on and sell out the honest men who had accepted him as one of them.

But, once, Teague had seen Les Jardeen walking arm in arm with Janet Sherrill under the stars and he had heard the girl laugh at some remark Jardeen had made. Not that she had had any real interest in Jardeen, at least not now. And now that she knew of his duplicity, she would hate him forever, for what he really was. But somehow Teague knew that a memory of Les Jardeen dying with a rope around his neck would be something very difficult for a girl like Janet Sherrill to forget.

Jim Teague headed for the Big Nugget as the most likely place to find Les Jardeen. Carrying through the evening air came the everlasting pound of the piano. Burnley was at it again, and now that weird music of discords was high and harsh, with a sort of desperate and savage urgency in the sound. Abruptly, just before Teague reached the door of the saloon, the nerve jangling music broke off on one final raw discord. When Teague stepped into the place, Burnley's seat at the piano was empty.

Strangely enough, except for the bartender, the whole place was empty, including the side room, the door of which was wide. Teague thought of what Jack Case had said. About the place being full of ghosts, ready to fly. And the nightly influx of miners had not yet begun.

Teague moved down along the bar, with the bartender eyeing him cautiously.

"Ides and Caldwell?" asked Teague brusquely. "Seen anything of them?"

Frank, the bartender, shook his head. "Not since they left before you were in here last, looking for them. Hell of a setup, this is. I don't know whether I'm afoot or horseback. If somethin' don't straighten out pretty damn quick, I'm takin' this apron off an' callin' it a day, myself."

"That," nodded Teague, "might be wise. Jardeen around?"

"Not for the past hour," answered Frank. "And he'll be wise if he never shows here again. Tod Burnley has taken just about all he's goin' to from that hombre. Which brings up something I been wantin' to tell you, Teague — just in case. Tod Burnley is a

232

damn good little man and he's the —"

Thud! Thud!

The two shots that echoed were muffled and heavy. The sounds came from outside the Big Nugget, on the upper side and toward the rear. Jim Teague spun around, taut and alert, and began moving toward the door.

Behind him the bartender sighed and said, "That's it, I reckon. I've seen it coming for a long time. And what I was aiming to tell you is that Tod Burnley is a good man and that Tess, his daughter, is a good girl, even if she does work the dance hall racket. Yeah, far too good a girl to run off with such as Les Jardeen, which is what Jardeen has been urgin' her to do. Well, Tod Burnley's been warnin' Jardeen over and over again to leave Tess alone, and I reckon Jardeen just had to learn the hard way that Tod meant business."

Gunfire, as always, had brought men running. Even by the time Jim Teague got out of the Big Nugget and around to that far corner, several miners were already bunched and pushing curiously about a crumpled figure. One of the miners was on his knee beside the figure. Now he straightened up, growling.

"Les Jardeen's as dead as he'll ever be.

233

One more of our kind done in by one of Caldwell's rotten crew. And there stands the one who did it!"

A little to one side stood the ugly, dwarfish figure of Tod Burnley, the piano player. In his hand he still held a stubby, but heavy-calibered derringer. He was impassive of face and he stood utterly still, clothed in a strange, quiet dignity. The miners began to move toward him menacingly. Jim Teague stepped in front of them, stopped them.

"Easy does it!" he warned crisply. "Things you don't know. Les Jardeen posed as being a miner. But he was really a Caldwell man, all the way. He was Caldwell's spy. He moved around among you, made the play of being Duff Sherrill's good friend, and all the time he was selling you out to Rupe Caldwell. This I know. If you don't believe me, ask Ben App or Barney Foxx. They'll tell you the same."

The miners paused, uncertain. One of them growled, "If Jardeen was another of Caldwell's crowd, what did this feller Burnley smoke him down for?"

"That," said Teague, "could be a personal matter between the two of them." He swung his glance to Burnley.

As he met Jim Teague's eyes, Burnley

234

said, "Any man has the right to protect the integrity of his own household. I stand on what I have done. My gun, sir — if you wish it."

He held the derringer toward Teague, butt foremost.

Teague shook his head. "Keep it," he said.

Tod Burnley, still cloaked in that strange dignity which made him seem a much bigger man physically than he actually was, inclined his head slightly. "Thank you," he said quietly. Then he turned and walked away.

Twilight had begun to thicken and a little breeze was pushing down from the Shawmuts. It was a good little breeze, clean and sweet with distance and with the breath of pine timber. Moving along the street, Jim Teague sucked it deep into his lungs, letting it wash all through him.

Nostalgia bit at him keenly, nostalgia for the open range and all the things he had known and loved best in his past life. The old impatience to be up and gone was working on him again, a yearning to get away from this Bonanza Gulch, where all was greed and deceit, it seemed. And where men died in tawdriness and without dignity.

Well, he didn't have to stay here; the way out was open enough to him. Yet he knew he would stay on, until this thing was fully settled, fully written, one way or the other. He thought wrily of another human frailty. Of this thing that some men called honor, but which also could be called stubborn pride. The issue between him and Rupe Caldwell was still open, still alive. And he had to see that issue settled, finally and for good, before he could ride out. When Rupe Caldwell's story in Bonanza Gulch was finally written and the last page turned, then he, Jim Teague, would go. That seemed the way the fates had willed this thing.

Lights were springing up around town. There was one glowing in the Sherrill cabin. Teague did not go that way. Instead he headed up to the group of three cabins which had housed Caldwell and his men. Two of the cabins were dark and empty. The third, Caldwell's own, and the one he had called home for a few days, was also dark, but not empty. Teague could smell the fresh cigarette smoke drifting from the open door. He paused, wary, hand sliding toward his gun.

"Who's inside?" he called harshly.

The answer was cold and quiet. "Riker."

"Alone?"

"Alone. Come in if you feel that way. We're both waiting for the same hombre, looks like."

Teague stepped in, caught the crimson wink of Rikers cigarette tip over on one of the bunks. Teague sat on the edge of the bunk across the room. "You seem sure that Caldwell will be back, Riker."

"He'll be back. But not figuring on staying, though he may be surprised, there. For the past several days I knew that Rupe Caldwell had it figured that the game was running out on him — running out fast! He wouldn't admit it openly, of course, for he liked that pose of being the biggest man in Bonanza Gulch, too big for anybody to touch him. But inside he knew, for in his way, he's smart about such things. But Rupe's always had one big weakness. He's greedy, greedy as hell. He hates to think of even an ounce of gold getting away from him. If he had a ton of the stuff, he'd want two tons. And he'll be thinking about how much a cleanup of his sluices would bring him. So he'll be back, after that cleanup gold."

"Then he's due for a big disappointment," drawled Teague. "The sluices have already been cleaned and the gold is with its rightful owner, Duff Sherrill."

"Hah!" murmured Wade Riker. "So you made that injunction stand up, eh? What a laugh that is on Judge Ormond, as well as on

Caldwell. For that injunction was never meant to be worth a damn, you know."

"That wasn't hard to figure right from the start," said Teague. Then he warned bluntly, "Don't say things you don't want made public knowledge. After all, I'm hardly a confidant of yours, Riker."

Riker laughed and there was no mirth in it. "Anything I say now you can spread as far as you want, Teague. If it puts a kink in Rupe Caldwell's tail, or anyone else who has it coming, for that matter, so much the better. I'll keep faith with any man who keeps faith with me. But I don't stand for any double-cross and I'm no fall guy in anybody's story book."

"Where would you say Caldwell and George Ides are now?" asked Teague.

"Somewhere back in the Shawmuts, getting everything fixed for the big ride. Something else you didn't know, Teague. Rupe's always had a little corral back in the timber, with horses in it and riding gear handy. So, any time he had immediate need for traveling, all he had to do was slip back into the timber on foot, slap a saddle on a bronc and be on his way. For all his brag and big talk, Rupe's been set to run, any time he had to. When he heard about Curly Bolan, he knew that time was here."

"Yet you figure he may show up again to-night?"

"I'm here, ain't I?" rapped Riker. "If I wasn't sure he'd be back, I'd be out figuring to trail him down."

"If and when he does show up, he'll no doubt have George Ides with him," reminded Teague. "And apparently Ides is pretty smooth with a gun."

"So am I," said Riker. Teague could almost sense the man's careless, confident shrug. "Ides is tough when he has the edge. But he won't have it with me. Neither will Caldwell. But, just in case one of them should shade me, here's a little more dope you're welcome to. Andy Carr never did sell Discovery to Rupe Caldwell. That bill of sale Caldwell has been flashing around, was written and signed by One Card Dan Ormond. And Caldwell changed the location of Andy Carr's original claim stake to frame an excuse for grabbing off Jack Dorgan's and Duff Sherrill's claims. But he still wasn't sure he could make it stick, so he tried to play safe by having Curly Bolan use that damned knife on Duff Sherrill. And when Jack Dorgan went on the prod in the Big Nugget, he played right into Caldwell's hands."

"Where's Andy Carr?" asked Teague.

"What became of him?"

Riker laughed again, harshly. "If you can't figure that one out for yourself, when at one time Caldwell had such as Bully Girard, Curly Bolan and George Ides and One Card Dan Ormond running loose and doing his bidding, then I'm not going to tell you. Now don't go asking me any more questions. You'll just be wasting your breath."

Teague got up, moved to the door. "You may have a long wait ahead of you, Riker."

"This is one wait I won't mind making, no matter how long it is," was the cold, impassive reply.

X

WHITE WATER

Jim Teague had his supper at the hashhouse and while he ate he thought about Wade Riker, dark and cold and inscrutable, waiting in that silent cabin with the stoic patience of an Indian. Waiting for Rupe Caldwell. Teague wondered what it was that had set Wade Riker off against Caldwell. Riker had alluded to a double-cross several times and had laid emphasis on Caldwell's greed. Most likely, Teague concluded, the trouble lay in some kind of argument over the division of the loot which Caldwell and his gang had piled up.

There was something else which Teague realized clearly. In a way, Wade Riker was just as culpable, just as much responsible for the crimes Caldwell's organization had committed as anyone else in the gang. Fully as much so as Les Jardeen had been. For the man had closed his eyes and made a mockery of the law he was supposed to represent and enforce. He had admitted his knowledge of the crooked manner Rupe

Caldwell had got hold of Andy Carr's Discovery claim and how he had tried to take over the claims of Duff, Sherrill and Jack Dorgan. He had also coldly suggested the fact that Andy Carr had been done away with and showed no concern over that fact.

Mulling these angles over in his mind, Teague knew that if he carried this word to Ben App and Barney Foxx, the vigilante group would move in on Riker. But despite the man's admitted depravity, Wade Riker was in some way a different breed from Caldwell and the rest. There was cold courage in this man and a scornful disregard for any danger that might come his way, either from Caldwell and Ides, or from the miners. The man might be a wolf, but he was certainly no coyote. And because of this, Teague could not deny a grudging respect for him.

Jack Case came into the eating house, slid onto the seat beside Teague. "Talked to a friend of yours just before dark, Jim," he murmured. "That Sherrill girl. She wants to see you. And say, what's this I hear about Les Jardeen?"

"If you hear that he's dead, that's true enough," answered Teague. "That fellow Burnley settled an old score. Jardeen learned the hard way that trying to play both ends against the middle can be suicide. And still there's no sign of Caldwell."

"Me," declared Jack Case, "I don't think there will be, either. My guess is that him and George Ides, seeing the way the cards were beginning to turn, have pulled out for good."

"It begins to look that way, all right," conceded Teague. "But I have the word of one man who knows Caldwell's makeup better than most, that Caldwell will be back. So I'm going to ride along with that hunch for a while."

"Supposin' he doesn't?" asked Case. "Suppose he really has lit a shuck — what are you going to do about it, Jim?"

Teague brooded a little over his coffee cup. "I can't give you a clear answer there, Jack. Haven't really thought things out that far . . . I've done all my planning on the hunch that Caldwell will show here once more, at least. If I'm wrong, and a day or two will show that, then I'll figure ahead."

"If Caldwell never comes back, you'd be wise to forget him," stated Case. "You've made your stand good. Caldwell made the threat, but you've outlasted him, Jim. He's the one who had to pull the run-out, not you."

"We'll see," nodded Teague briefly. "But

for a time at least, keep prowling and watch-ing, Jack. Caldwell can show again just as suddenly as he disappeared."

Sauntering down to the Sherrill cabin under the early stars, Jim Teague thought of how, even in the relatively short time he'd been in Bonanza Gulch, the season had mellowed. Though at this elevation the nights would always be crisp and sharp, at the same time the final hard, bitter edge of a departed winter had almost completely van-ished. The fullness of spring was at hand and the world stirred to its gathering benefi-cence, throbbed to its ripening vitality.

And, while the plains were his chosen des-tiny, this was good country, too. For that matter, he mused, there was never anything really wrong with any kind of wilderness in itself. It was man and his works that made the difference. The whole fault always lay with what men did, what they built and what they destroyed. Even so, time whipped all men in the end. Given time enough and the wilderness would take over once more. Given time, and the staunchest building in Bonanza Gulch would moulder to nothing. As for the gouging and burrowings of men down in the diggings, a few short years, a freshet or two and all these would be rolled over and smoothed out and then the gulch would be its eternal perfect self once more.

Teague smiled grimly into the darkness. When a man's thoughts began running this way, he decided, it was either a sign that he was growing old, or that he was just awakening to the really significant things in life. He was either all through, or he was just beginning to build on the promise of the future.

He knocked on the Sherrill door and it was Janet who opened it for him. The warm flavor of right and decent living came out of this humble cabin and enveloped him with its goodness. The girl's eyes were shining, her face bright. Her hands came out impulsively and rested in his.

"Jim!" she exclaimed softly. "I'm so glad you've come. Dad and I, we want to thank you for all you've done for us. I don't know what we'd have ever done if it wasn't for you."

Teague was amazed at the change in Duff Sherrill, who seemed twenty years younger. The grizzled miner got up and wrung Teague's hand heartily.

"I've been trying to think of all the things I've got to apologize to you for, Teague," he rumbled. "But whatever they are, consider it done."

Apparently, neither of the Sherrills had as yet heard of Les Jardeen's violent and tawdry finish, and Teague was glad of that. This cabin had had enough shadows thrown over it. He took a chair and let his big shoulders sag in complete rest. The gaunt bleakness of his face softened and the girl, watching, saw the strong, warm vitality of youth come into his eyes and take the sternness from about his lips.

To Duff Sherrill, Teague said, "You owe me neither thanks or apologies. To be welcome in a cabin like this, well, that more than pays for everything." His glance touched the girl as he said this and warm color washed across her face.

"That claim of mine," said Sherrill. "I know now, from that one cleanup you and the boys made in the sluices, that it will provide the means for all the things I've always wanted to see my girl have in life. Comfort, a real home, security — all such things. Providing I can hang onto the claim, of course."

"You'll hang on to it, Mr. Sherrill," Teague assured him. "I know for a fact now that you had everything figured just about right. Andy Carr never did sell to Rupe Caldwell. He never wrote that bill of sale, which was an out-and-out forgery. A fellow named One Card Dan wrote it. As for Andy Carr, well, that's one more thing Rupe Caldwell has to answer for."

"You mean that Caldwell had Andy Carr done away with?" Sherrill asked.

Teague nodded. "I'm afraid that's about right."

He saw Duff Sherrill's lips tighten, saw a shadow take some of the glow from the girl's eyes. Which Teague hated to see, but it was a conclusion that they would have had to come to, in the end. Just like they would hear about Les Jardeen and there wasn't anything he could do about that, either. So he changed the subject.

"And when you've taken all the gold out of your claim that it will yield, Mr. Sherrill, what then? You won't be staying in Bonanza Gulch?"

"Hardly!" said Sherrill explosively. "There's a place I know about over in the Antelope River country where the bottom land runs deep and rich on each side of the river. Land that was meant to grow things. All my life I've dug in the earth, looking for gold. And all my life I've wanted to dig in the earth to make things grow. Fruit trees, berry vines, grain. And though this may sound queer coming from a miner, I've had a yearning to see a bunch of white-faced cattle grazing, cattle bearing my brand. Yeah, I got plenty of plans ahead for Janet and myself."

A brooding look came into Teague's eyes. "You draw a pretty picture, sir. I envy you. Most men dream. A few manage to make their dreams come true. So many of them never do. There seems to be —"

He broke off, listening. Outside came the pound of running boots, then a hard, urgent knocking at the door. Teague jumped up and opened it. Jack Case stood there.

"Caldwell's back, Jim," panted Case. "Just saw him ride in, him and George Ides. They turned up toward Caldwell's cabin!"

Teague said, "Be right with you, Jack." He turned to the Sherrill's. "Sorry I got to leave you again so quickly, folks. But I've got things to do."

He had stepped out into the night when Janet Sherrill's soft cry reached him. "Jim! Wait — !"

He turned as she came darting through the doorway. Jack Case, with fine discernment, moved off a little way into the dark. The girl caught at Teague's arms, holding him, standing close to him. "You've done so much already, Jim. Do you have to go after Caldwell? Can't someone else handle this?"

"Someone may," he told her, thinking of Wade Riker, dark-faced and stoic, waiting in Caldwell's cabin. "But I've got to make sure. You mustn't worry over me. I'm nothing, really."

"You're more than you think — to me, Jim Teague." Her voice went small, tear-choked. "Oh, Jim — come back — !"

He put her aside, wordless, gentle. Then he hurried away into the night, with Jack Case falling into step with him.

"They came in pretty sly and soft," said Case. "I was lucky. Just happened to see 'em slipping by in back of the trading post. No swagger and bully puss to them now. No heading straight in to the Big Nugget, full of brass and confidence. No, the wolves have turned coyote, now. And they'll spook easy."

In the cabin, Wade Riker was building another of the endless string of cigarettes he'd smoked since starting his lonely and vengeful wait. But as the soft thump of hoofs sounded through the night, his fingers stilled, then dropped paper and tobacco. He came up off the bunk, moved a little way toward the center of the room.

He heard saddle girths creak as men dismounted in front of the cabin, heard a low murmur of voices. Then the figures of two men showed, one behind the other at the doorway. The one in the lead was Rupe Caldwell and he stopped suddenly, smelling that tobacco smoke. His voice rang in taut, harsh alarm.

"Who's in here?"

"Riker," came the cold answer. "Don't wink an eye, Rupe. I got a gun on you!"

Caldwell froze, and his tone went thin and strained. "What's wrong, Wade? What's the idea of the gun? Hell, man — I got plans —"

"Sure," cut in Riker, "sure you have, Rupe. But I got some of my own. Been waiting to tell you about them. You're ready to cut and run from this place, and I know it. But what about my share of the loot you've been gathering? I was to get my fifth cut of it. What about that?"

"That's why I'm here, Wade," argued Caldwell. "I was aiming to hunt you up. You and me and George, we're going to clean up the sluice boxes, empty the safe in my office and then hit the trail. The three of us, we'll divide it all three ways."

"Rupe," droned Riker, "you don't even tell a good lie. There's no gold in your office safe. You know damned well that you cleaned that out. I've watched you open that safe often enough to know how to do it myself. So, after you disappeared so sudden and mysterious, I figured I better take a look in that safe. You know what I found — not a single ounce of gold. You'd already seen to that."

The lock of Wade Riker's gun snicked as he drew the hammer fully back. "Yeah," he went on, in that same toneless way, "that safe was empty. You'd already cleaned the gold out of that. So now you're back to make a cleanup of the sluice boxes. Well, you can forget about that. The sluices have already been cleaned, by the same bunch that lynched Curly Bolan. You came back after an empty sack, Rupe. Not a damn thing in it but me. But I'm enough. You were out to double-cross me, Rupe — like you'd double-cross your own mother. You're a slimy snake and not fit to live. Which is a little thing I'm taking care of, now!"

Peering past Rupe Caldwell's shoulder, George Ides had been plotting, with a terrible, strained intensity, Wade Riker's exact position in the blackness of the cabin. Ides had nothing to go by but the droning of Riker's voice, and he knew by the way Riker's tone was thinning and pinching down that in another second or two he would start shooting.

Ides had inched his own gun free, had shoved it past Caldwell's hip and now, as near as he could tell, it was lined right. He pulled the trigger as Riker's last word was given out in emphatic flatness. George Ides never took a longer gamble, nor one that paid off so well. His bullet took Riker squarely in the center of the chest.

The shock threw Riker back and he started to go down. He shot three times while falling, but the shock of Ides' bullet had knocked all ordinary reflex and coordination out of him and his lead flew wild. Rupe Caldwell, knowing the bursting flood of relief of one reprieved, snatched his gun and blazed a savage shot or two across the cabin's blackness. Then he whirled and his voice rang harshly.

"This smells like a trap! Let's get out of here, George!"

Jim Teague and Jack Case had reached that single crooked street of Bonanza Gulch and were crossing it, angling toward the slope where Caldwell's cabin stood, when out ahead of them the night shook and shuddered with that rolling drum of gunfire.

They broke into a run, driving for the cabin, closing in on it fast. In the dark ahead a nervous horse snorted and trampled. Then they heard Rupe Caldwell's cry: "Let's get out of here, George!"

A horse grunted under the biting urge of savage spurring. Jim Teague lifted a taunting yell.

"What you running for, Rupe?"

His answer was a curse and the whip of gunfire. Beside him, Jack Case grunted and went down, a leg buckling under him.

Case swore thinly, then urged, "Go ahead, Jim — go ahead! It's just a leg — !"

Teague kept going and was almost run down by the bulk of two horses, hurtling past at full speed. In fact a stirrup, flaring and solid under the press of a rider's stiffened leg, did catch him slightly, spinning him half around. At the same instant a gun blared almost in his face, so close that the lurid flame of it nearly scorched him. He marveled that the bullet had missed. But that gun flame left his eyes momentarily shocked and blinded and, though he threw shot after shot at those fleeing riders, he knew he was doing no good, for at the moment he could see nothing and the impact of that stirrup still had him off balance.

He got his feet solidly under him again and ran on toward the cabin, scrubbing a hand across his eyes, trying to clear them. He bumped into the cabin wall, found the door and called, "Riker! Wade Riker!"

He hardly expected an answer. The acrid bite of gun smoke lay thick in the cabin, stung his nostrils.

Came a faint stir and then a voice, equally faint. "Teague! That you, Teague? Joke's —

on me. Should have shot first — and talked after. But I wanted Caldwell to know — why he was gettin' it. It was Ides — got me. He shot at my voice. Man's a fool — to talk too much — !"

Wade Riker's voice thinned and faded. Teague found him, crumpled there on the cabin floor. He dropped on his knees beside Riker. "Hang on, man!" he urged. "I'll get a light — !"

"No need, Teague," came the answer, very faint but strangely steady, now. "Light won't reach where I'm goin'. You're wastin' time. You ought to be — after them. It's night — plenty dark. Trail won't be — easy to follow. Try White Water — east of Blizzard Pass. I was to get a fifth — of the loot. Caldwell was out to take it all — double-cross me. Shouldn't have talked. Should have shot first — and then taken it all. White Water — !"

Teague straightened, got a match going, found the lamp and lighted it. He knew a deep relief. His eyes were clearing and he could see properly again.

Wade Riker was shot through and through. Teague thought he was gone, but there was a final stir of life left in this dark-faced, unreadable man.

"White Water," whispered Riker again.

"That's where Caldwell would have hid the stuff — I think. The cave on White Water. I talked too much — first time in my life and it was my — big mistake. Should have shot first. White Water, Teague — you'll find them — there. Good — luck — !"

Wade Riker gave a long, shivering sigh and seemed to shrink. And Jim Teague knew that now indeed had Riker gone.

Teague went outside, heard men moving and calling about town. And he heard Jack Case, still swearing out there in the dark. Teague went to him, got the wounded Case across his shoulder and carried him down to the stage station.

Ben App was there, to help Teague get Jack Case as comfortable as possible while a stage station hand set out to round up Doc Beals, a dissolute old reprobate who, if reasonably sober, could still do a first-class job on an injured man. Ben App gave Case a long pull from a private bottle and then turned to Teague for explanations. While Teague was telling him, Barney Foxx and Tim McCord came hurrying in, and then there was Duff Sherrill, using his cane.

Teague gave them what he knew. Barney Foxx cursed and growled, "We'll get a posse together and go after them."

"Go where, Barney?" asked Teague. "And

what good is a posse, stumbling and floundering through the timber? No, this is a one-man job and I'm taking it."

"Why should you, Jim?" asked Duff Sherrill. "You've done your share. None of the gold they got away with was your gold. Let those who've taken the loss go it from here."

Teague shook his head, his face pulled and cold. "There's Jack Case yonder, with a bad leg. And then there's a thing between Caldwell and me. If he rides clear now, he wins. And I'd always be restless over that. No, I'm going after him. Who knows where a place called White Water is?"

It was Tim McCord who answered this. "There's a creek called White Water, east of Blizzard Pass. It runs down the south slope of the Shawmuts, through a deep, narrow canyon. Never heard of any other place than that by that name."

"Is there a cave in that canyon?" asked Teague.

Tim McCord shrugged. "Wouldn't know. Never been through it. But there could be. The canyon walls are steep and broken enough."

"I'll have a look at it," said Teague briefly. "Ben, I'll want that horse and outfit again."

"Yours, of course," nodded Ben.

The stage station roustabout returned with Doc Beals, a short, paunchy man, a little frowsy, face pouched from over-indulgence with a whiskey bottle. But he was more than half sober and he took over with brusque professionalism. Teague moved up to the bunk where Jack Case lay, gripped Case's hand.

"Make a good ride of it, Jack. You'll be all right."

"Sure," said Case, grinning tightly, "Sure, Jim. Same to you. Wish I was going with you. But don't make the same mistake Riker did."

"I won't. I'll do my talking with something besides words."

Teague went out with Ben App, who carried a lantern. Tim McCord went with them. Teague took the same horse he'd had in running down Curly Bolan. Not a particularly fast horse, but a staunch and mountainwise one, reliable and with plenty of bottom.

"That White Water Creek, Jim," said Tim McCord, "you can't miss it. Go straight east from the pass. You'll hit a big aspen swamp and the creek rises there, from a spring. I know that much about it, but I don't know what you'll find in the canyon. I've never been closer than the rim."

"Bring that lantern, Ben," said Teague as he started off, leading his horse.

They went up to Caldwell's cabin and from there, using the lantern light, followed the deep-cut, plunging hoof-marks made by the horses of Caldwell and Ides when they fled the town. They followed these until they saw the sign cut definitely into the Blizzard Pass road. Then Teague swung astride, saying briefly, "Be seeing you, gents."

"Damn it, Jim — I hate to see you go alone," argued Ben App. "A bad pair of hombres you're after."

"Better this way, Ben," Teague told him. "One man who understands this sort of business, can do better than a dozen who don't. He can travel faster and more quietly and keep better hidden. I'm not worrying."

"Maybe not," grumbled Ben App. "But I am and I will be, until I see you again. Good luck, Jim!"

The midnight stars hung low and bright and cold. The hoofs of Jim Teague's horse were a muffled beat in the dust of the Blizzard Pass road. Teague's progress had been fairly slow, up the long climb of the road. Nothing was truer, he knew, than the old saying about a stern chase being a long one. And this was a trail to be sure about, every step of the way. One mistake could be disastrous.

It was reasonable to believe that Rupe Caldwell and George Ides, realizing that their game in Bonanza Gulch had completely run out for them, would be mainly concerned in a swift getaway with all the golden treasure which they had, by fair means and foul, gotten together. At the same time there was always a chance that somewhere along this road, they might lie in wait to ambush any possible pursuit. So it was wise to go slowly and make sure.

From time to time along the way, Jim Teague had reined in, got out of the saddle, scratched a match and surveyed the road's surface, now deep-rutted and dusty from the churning wheels of stage and freight wagon. Each time he had seen the marks of two horses, still moving up. So now he stopped for another such look.

Before lighting the match he listened and keened the night with every taut sense. The slope of the Shawmuts was vast and black, still and sleeping. So Teague snapped the match alight and had his look. The fresh hoof-marks were still there, still leading upward. What he was after was to make sure he did not override a turn-off that Caldwell and Ides might make at any time.

Back on his horse, Teague went on, musing that a man, used to the saddle, was only half complete when he was out of it. And though there was no telling what lay ahead of him, it was good to be up and moving, to know that the trail was narrowing down and that somewhere ahead lay a final accounting.

Yet, for all his care, Teague overshot the turn-off. For when he made another stop, about a mile short of Blizzard Pass, and searched the road for sign, there were no fresh horse-tracks showing. Teague straightened, pinched out the match and looked back down along the mountain's dark flank.

It was big, this country, measured in tens of long running miles. This was, he realized grimly, no easy task he had set himself to. These mountains held thousands of out-of-the-way spots where men might hide. Daylight, of course, would have simplified matters a great deal. Then it would be no trick at all to retrace the road until he found the point of turnoff — but could he afford to wait for daylight?

Caldwell and Ides had headstart enough as it was. Every added hour of time that they got would see them that much further on their way, add to his own difficulties in catching up with them. And in daylight they could watch their back trail much better.

Jim Teague realized that he had to

gamble. He had to gamble that when Wade Riker had said that White Water was the place to look, he had given the right steer. Dark and secretive as the rogue sheriff had been, it was logical that the man, with his last words, had spoken the truth. He would have wanted to get even with Rupe Caldwell above everything else. And the only way he could hope to do this was to speak the truth.

Caldwell had made Riker promises of big reward, just as he had made them to Teague himself. That was Caldwell's way of binding men to him, getting them to serve his ends. And when they had done this, when their use to him was done and when Caldwell considered them too little or weak to harm him, he tossed them aside. Or, if they were of stern stuff and dangerous, Caldwell had them rubbed out.

Teague thought of Bully Girard and his sawed-off shotgun. That was the way Rupe Caldwell worked. And Wade Riker — smart enough to have seen this was what Caldwell intended for him too, but not smart enough to get there first — had said to head for White Water. It was the only sound lead for Jim Teague to follow, now. So he took it.

He rode up into the very gut of Blizzard Pass before he left the road. He ferreted a way through the gaunt rock rims that guarded the pass and headed east, riding slowly. Tim McCord had told him he couldn't miss running into the headwaters of White Water Creek if he did this. So he sighted the stars and kept to that steady, careful pace, letting his horse feel its way along this backbone of the world.

The hours and the miles drifted and then dawn began to peek over the rim of the world and look Jim Teague in the eye. But there was more than dawnlight in the air. There was sound, also, the muffled, steady roar of water, running fast and pounding out a droning echo against rock and ledge. Ahead, the misted crown of the mountain top sloped swiftly into deeper shadow. Ahead lay a canyon. This should be White Water.

Jim Teague moved carefully up to the rim. Below lay blackness and out of it boiled the steady thunder of lashing waters. The air lifting from the rumbling depths was damp, smelling of mists and spray. Teague got out of the saddle, hunkered down and built a cigarette. He cupped a match carefully and briefly in his hands, inhaling deeply. There was nothing more to do now but wait for full daylight.

It came slowly, grayly at first, then changing to warmer, more delicate coloring. Detail began to grow, timber tops take individual form. What had been merely a dark patch of substance off to Teague's right, now resolved itself into a clump of tamaracks, fringed with chokeberry and wild plum.

A whistling snort and a startled stamping told of a big mule deer buck, on its way to morning browse, catching the foreign scent of man and horse, and bounding away to deeper security. The smell of timber, gathered in potency during the still, moist night hours, filled a man's lungs with aromatic breath.

The pink of the eastern sky became a rose which deepened and brightened to a fiery consistency. Near at hand a pine sparrow tried a few tentative notes, then sang lustily. Banners of light began fanning up from beyond the edge of the eastern world, building a great and towering radiance. This was day.

Jim Teague stirred, got to his feet and led his horse behind the shelter of the tamarack thicket. Then, afoot, he moved into the open and let his glance run, measuring and intent. He saw movement in many places, but it all belonged to the wilderness. Deer feeding. The swift gray shadow of a timber wolf, come and gone in a sliding flash. A hawk on a dead pine snag, spreading its wings, making ready for another day of soaring hunt. But there was no sign or move of what Teague was looking for. From all immediate signs he was the only human to watch the dawn take over this part of the Shawmut Mountains.

To his right the canyon dropped away and away, winding down the southern flank of the Shawmuts. To his left lay a wilderness of tamarack and aspen thickets, of chokeberry and snow brush, with upthrust rock spines jabbing through here and there in a wild, broken confusion. This was stern country in which to hunt for the trails of wary and dangerous men.

Teague went back to his horse and cut north, riding with extreme caution. It was a slow and twisting way he had to take, breaking through the lesser thickets, circling the thicker ones and skirting rock outcrops. And always the need of senses alert and straining.

He crossed faint trails, but all were game trails. He moved on to the north until the country started dropping down ahead of him, where the rocky summit began once more to give way to timber. Teague realized that he had crossed the crest of the Shawmuts once more and was now at the beginning of the north flank of the mountains, and had found nothing of what he was searching for.

Doubt rose and deepened in him. It did not make sense that Wade Riker had lied to him. Dying men, vengeful to the last, would not lie to thwart that very vengeance they thirsted for. They might lie to fulfill it, but not to deny it.

Teague studied the rank timber below him and, as he did so, knew a fresh idea. Coming in from Blizzard Pass along the extreme rocky backbone of the mountains as he had done, was slow and tricky going. But if a man, knowing the country well, had left the road below the pass and cut up through the timber at a slant, he'd have made much better time and known an easier trail. He would have been taking a short cut to his destination. Rupe Caldwell and George Ides, knowing this country, would have had that figured.

Teague rode straight down through the timber, where the cold morning shadows still held deep and silent. And within three hundred yards Teague cut fresh horse sign. Two horses, moving east but also upward at a long slant through the timber. Teague slid his rifle out of the scabbard, carried it ready across his saddle. He set his horse to the same trail. Wade Riker had not lied or given a false steer.

Before long the timber began to thin again as the summit neared once more. Here the trail skirted the summit tangle, holding to the comparatively open edge of the timber. The sun was fully up, now, lancing the timber with gold. Teague pulled his hat low, peered through the growing blaze.

The trail swung upward, climbing through a shallow saddle where the silver boles of quaking aspen speared the darker green. The trail crossed here, and then beyond there was a spreading aspen swamp and ground that was soggy under foot and spring water dripping and swirling into a water course beyond. Here, exactly as Tim McCord had described it, lay the source of White Water Creek.

The sign Teague was following circled the edge of the aspen swamp, crossed the quickening headwaters of the creek at a shallows and dropped into the head of the canyon beyond.

Jim Teague paused for another long moment. This was the canyon of White Water that he was about to enter. Where this trail would lead him he did not know. What he would meet down there somewhere ahead, he could only guess at. But this was White Water. He set himself a trifle more solidly in the saddle, touched his horse with the spur.

XI

FOR SOME THE SUN

The canyon way dropped swiftly and within a couple of hundred yards the walls had already lifted a full hundred feet above the trail and the wet, shadowy way ahead grew deeper with every stride of Jim Teague's horse.

This was wild, lonely country. Here, what with the ever-deepening growl of tumbling surging water and with canyon walls rising loftier all the time, a rifle shot would be a puny sound indeed, quickly smothered and absorbed. Here a man could die, swiftly and violently and his bones moulder to dust without ever being seen by another of his kind. Here a man could be trapped, wiped out without trace.

The icy breath of extreme and deadly danger breathed across Jim Teague's nerve ends, leaving them ruffed and electric. The straining alertness he was forcing from every sense in him was a pressure at the back of his neck, a weight behind his eyes. He was riding into something here, of his own free will and choice. Why?

There was no personal gain in this for him. Caldwell had stolen no gold from him. The men who had died at the hands of Caldwell's men or at his bidding, men like Jack Dorgan, Claus Lehrmann, Bob Porter — the driver and shotgun guard of the stage — these were all men whom Jim Teague had never seen before coming to Bonanza Gulch, and he had known none of them personally. Wade Riker had been victim of his own dark partnership, such a one as Teague himself had so narrowly escaped being drawn into. So why was he, Jim Teague, here? Maybe it was just one of those things that was written. . . .

Deeper and deeper dropped the canyon, higher and higher climbed its walls. There was one comforting angle about the situation. A man need not watch anywhere but ahead. For to Teague's right were the lashing creek waters, beating and battering at bare, black rocks. To his left the east wall rose, sheer and abrupt. In many places as he rode along, Teague could have reached out a hand and touched that sheer wall. So always he kept his glance reaching and probing ahead and below.

Most of the trail was rocky, but here and there a spread of wet and shallow earth lay and in these places the marks of two horses cut plainly, heading ever deeper into this gloomy tangle of white water and black shadow.

He came to a place where the canyon wall bulged outward and the trail narrowed until it hung almost directly over the churning, rumbling creek waters. But beyond the bulge the canyon wall gave back into a narrow, rock-walled cleft, running almost at a direct angle from the main canyon. Into that cleft the horse sign turned.

The break in the canyon wall wound crookedly, climbing slightly. From the far side of the canyon a man might have glimpsed the mouth of the break, but could have seen but little way into it and so would have guessed it to have no greater depth than that. Even a man, riding this faint trail and following no leading sign, could have ridden past the spot and thought nothing of it, so deceptively did its inner twistings hide the true reach of it. But this sign Teague was looking at did not lie. Two horses had gone into the twisting depths of the cleft and had not come out.

Here at the mouth of the cleft was space enough for a horse to stand with security, so Teague left his mount there and moved into the cleft's dank gloom afoot. The booming of the creek waters was an aid, here. For any sound of a man's movements was as nothing against that solid beat.

A trickle of water sluiced its way underfoot, leading out to the parent stream. Here was all dark shadow and moist chill. The sun would not touch this spot until almost directly overhead, and then but briefly. Jim Teague followed a right-hand twist, then a left, and finally another turn to the right where the way narrowed to a distance of scarcely two yards across. But beyond that spot the rocky walls gave back into a little basin perhaps fifty yards wide. Down through a space of time measured by untold millions of years, water and wind, sun and ice had worked at a core of rock softer than that surrounding it, had dissolved and scoured and eroded it, until this little basin had been sculptured out, the remains washed out through the cleft into the creek below. And now Jim Teague, glancing across the place, saw that which brought him up on his toes, his rifle swiftly lifting.

Out there in the basin stood two horses. One of them, with a nose bag already in place, was munching hungrily at a measure of oats. The other was reaching eagerly for a bag about to be hung in place by a slender figure that was dapper, even in these wild surroundings. George Ides!

It would have been simple enough for Jim Teague to have cut down Ides then and there, for the man stood with his back to Teague. And Teague knew that were their situations reversed, Ides would not hesitate a fraction of a second. But, much as Ides had forfeited all right to any fair break, it wasn't in Teague to cut him down in this manner. So Teague stepped slightly into the clear and his voice rang sharply across the distance between them, for here, in the basin, the rumble of the creek waters was muted.

"You can quit cold, Ides — or you can go for it. The choice is yours!"

Giving George Ides any chance at all was a mistake. Wade Riker was dead because he'd made such a mistake. And Jim Teague knew flashing wonder if he had erred also. For with the speed of a startled cat, Ides came around, hand flashing for his gun. He had the weapon out and stabbing level as Jim Teague pulled the trigger of his rifle. The bellow of the rifle lifted just ahead of the shorter, flatter bark of Ides' hand gun.

Jim Teague felt the breath of Ides' slug past his cheek, heard it smash into the solid rock behind him. His own rifle bullet, heavy and lethal, whirled Ides completely off his feet, dropping him in a crumpled heap. The voice of the rifle beat up the encircling cliffs in a roll of heavy reverberation.

Even as he swung the lever of his rifle, pumping in another shell, Teague was racing across the basin, past the shrunken figure of George Ides, past the startled and whirling horses. For at the far side of the basin, above two shallow, step-like ledges, stood a huge segment of rock which had, at some ancient past time, plunged from the cliff above. Beyond the rock was a dark opening in the cliff wall. Teague lunged up and across the ledges and threw himself against the sheltering base of the rock. There he waited.

Beyond the rock he heard movement. He smelled wood smoke and the aroma of frying bacon. A pan clanged on rock and it was Rupe Caldwell's voice calling. "George — George — !"

Teague answered. "You'll have to do without Ides, Rupe. It's all thinned down to just you and me, now. One guess as to who's talking, Rupe!"

"Teague!" The word burst from Rupe Caldwell's lips like a strangled curse. Then came real cursing, a fury of it, wild and strained. "You'll have to come and get me, Teague!"

"All in good time, Rupe — all in good

time," mocked Teague. "There's only one way out of this place, it seems, and you'll have to get past me to reach it. And I got lots of patience, Rupe — lots of it. The day is young yet, but time will pass. And when it gets dark, why then I'll be coming in after you. And I won't be talking, Rupe — like Wade Riker was; I'll be shootin'."

Came another fury of cursing and Teague nodded to himself at the shrillness of it. He'd heard that note in the voices of men before, men trapped and desperate and their nerves taut to breaking. Teague taunted him some more.

"Once there was a man who thought he was so big he could do as he pleased and that nothing could touch him. Bear with me, Rupe, and listen to the little story. Yeah, this guy — and it was you, Rupe — kidded himself into believing he was big, awful big. He set out to loot a gold camp. He lied and cheated and double-crossed. And he figured other men were too dumb and slow-brained ever to understand. But he made a lot of mistakes. First off, he played me for a sucker, and nearly made a go of it. When he found he'd failed, he set Bully Girard after me with a shotgun. And then he thought he'd left Wade Riker dead. But Riker lived a while, long enough to tell me about this place. He figured this was where you'd head to, to hide out for a while, and he told me about it. So I'm here, Rupe — waiting for you."

There was no answer from Caldwell. Teague went on. "I'm not here alone, Rupe. Andy Carr is here with me, and Jack Dorgan. Then there's Claus Lehrmann and Bob Porter. You didn't think. you could ever get away from them, did you, Rupe?"

There was no tremor in this rock. It was too massive, too solidly set with time. But to a man crouched close against it, it carried sound, the faintest of scraping. Jim Teague heard and understood. He edged backward, foot by foot until he was fully in the angle formed by the inner end of the rock and the base of the cliff. There, a good two yards from where he had been, he waited.

He saw the muzzle of the gun first, inching past the top of the rock, then the full barrel and the action and the hand that was gripping it. Abruptly the head and shoulders of Rupe Caldwell lunged into view, his arm dropping over the edge of the rock while he hammered shot after shot straight down at the place below, where Jim Teague had first been crouched.

"Wrong place, Rupe!" said Teague, as he pulled the trigger of his rifle.

Back in Bonanza Gulch, Ben App glanced at the slim figure of Janet Sherrill as she poised in the doorway of the stage station. Ben spoke, gently reproving.

"Now you're just fretting yourself unnecessary, Miss Janet. Jim Teague will make out all right. He's the sort who'll always make out all right in anything he sets himself to do. He's a lot bigger man than he realizes, Jim is. He knows how to take care of himself. Why, Jack Casc, he told me that not one man in a hundred — yes, in a thousand — could have acted and thought fast enough to come out of that Bully Girard affair with a whole skin. I tell you, there's no need of worrying about Jim Teague."

"But he left way last night," argued the girl. "And here it is, coming on night again. And he's not back and there's no word of him."

"Pshaw! What of that?" scoffed Ben App. "Maybe the trail didn't lead to where Wade Riker said it would. Wherever it leads, you can bet Jim Teague will find it and follow it. Look how he trailed down Curly Bolan. And you want to remember that Caldwell and Ides had quite a start on him. So now you just run along home and get supper going for your father. He'll need it after fussing around those sluice boxes of his claim all day. And him not too long out of a sick bed. Though I got to admit he's come back awful fast and strong, now he's sure of the claim once more. I promise, soon as I get word from Jim, I'll let you know."

The girl hesitated, looked off into the deepening twilight, then nodded. "I'll be waiting."

Soberness came over Ben App when she had gone. "You're a damned hypocrite, Ben App," he admitted to himself. "You're mighty worried about Jim Teague yourself. For that girl's sake, more than anything else, Jim — I'm sure hoping you come back to us."

It was a half hour later that Ben App heard plodding hoofs coming in through the early, crisp dark. He hurried out, caught the bulk of them against the early stars. Three horses, one with a rider, the others weary under heavy packs.

"Jim!" called the stage agent. "Jim Teague!"

"That's right, Ben," came the answer, subdued and weary. "Come here and take over. Here's the damned gold. It's all yours. I want no part of it. It's cost enough — in blood. That canvas poke that Claus Lehrmann had was in with the rest. When I saw that, then I felt a little better about what I had to do to get it. They had it cached in a cave in White Water canyon, just like Wade Riker said. I brought in all there was of it."

Ben App made several trips back and forth before he got it all off those two led horses, until only empty saddles remained and the horses sighed in deep content to be rid of their dead-weight burdens of yellow treasure. And he identified most of it, for it was still in its original pokes.

"Here's what was taken in that stage robbery!" he exclaimed. "And you're right, Jim — this was Claus Lehrmann's poke. I still got that letter that Claus never lived to read. The address of the lady who wrote it is on the envelope. I'll see that the full value of the poke goes to her."

Not until he had it all sorted and much of it identified by names and initials scrawled on the buckskin and heavy canvas bags, did Ben App think of other things. Then he asked, "Caldwell and Ides — what about them, Jim?"

Teague stood leaning against a doorpost, his big shoulders sagging, his face dark and bleak. "You can forget about them," he answered stonily. Then he added, in a brooding undertone, "I hope I can." He squared himself a little. "Where's Jack Case?"

"Back in my living quarters and doing all

right. And say, that nice Sherrill girl has been plenty worried about you, Jim. I told her I'd let her know just as soon as you came in. Maybe you ought to take the word to her yourself."

Teague did not answer, but crossed the room and went back into Ben App's living quarters, where he found Jack Case propped up on a bunk, smoking interminable cigarettes. Case looked pretty good and his eyes brightened in the lamplight as Teague came in.

"About time," he said gruffly. "You're the first person I ever worried about besides myself. You got 'em?"

Teague nodded.

"I knew you would," growled Case. "There's some the sun shines for and you're one of them. What now, Jim? Set your sights high. You're too big a man to start drifting again."

"I'm no different than I was when I hit this camp," said Teague wearily. "A little older, a little wiser. And with a few more memories — not all of them good. That's all I got, Jack."

"No, not all — not near all," Case differed. "You've moved into the lives of people who count. You've shaken down into something substantial and real and plenty worth while. I know the kind of shadows you're prowling through now. But you'll climb out of them. And then you'll realize that I know what I'm talking about. I recommend the smiles of that little Sherrill girl. They'll cure you quicker than anything else."

"I own," said Teague slowly, "just what you see on me. I haven't another thing to my name."

"Hell with that talk!" snorted Jack Case in exasperation. "You own your future, don't you? I wish I had one that promised as much. You can make that future anything you want. Now get out of here. Even if this cussed leg of mine does hurt like billy-be-damned, I think I can get some sleep, now."

Jim Teague went out into the night. He was hungry, yet he did not want to eat. He was weary, yet he did not want to rest. He looked down toward the Sherrill cabin. There was a warm and somehow beckoning light shining from its window, which drew him in spite of himself.

He knocked softly, but the door was wide in an instant. And there she stood, unable to speak for a moment, twisting her slim hands. Then she said it all in one little sobbing cry.

"Jim!"

She was in his arms, clinging to him, and he was dumb and motionless with the wonder of it.

Now it was Duff Sherrill, fumbling and mumbling as he edged past them, and his mumbling was something about having to see Ben App, for he knew Ben would have a lot to tell him. . . .

Janet Sherrill drew Teague into the cabin, shut the door, then crept into his arms again. Teague was still searching for words. He found some finally, stumbling over them a little. "I haven't a thing to offer you, except myself, girl. I own no gold claim, no ranch — nothing. I'm just as I stand here, with the smell of gun smoke on me —"

She laughed up at him through her tears. "All I want is you — just as you are. But there's Dad's dream of that ranch. And my dream where I'll have both of you. Isn't that enough, Jim?"

Jim Teague, in some new and deep and contented wisdom, knew that it was.